THE COLDEST DECEMBER

THE COLDEST DECEMBER

a Short Story Collection
to Remember the Halifax Explosion
by Nova Scotia Authors

Quarter Castle Publishing
December 6, 2017
Nova Scotia, Canada

ISBN (eBook): 978-1-927625-28-6
ISBN (paperback): 978-1-927625-27-9

Cover Design: Diana Tibert
Interior Design: Diana Tibert

Cover Images
1 Front: City of Tents (No 3905, page 25): Taken January 5, 1918
Link: https://commons.wikimedia.org/wiki/
File:No_3905_Page_25,_cit%C3%A9_des_tentes.jpg

2 Front: Tufts Cove School, Tufts Cove, Dartmouth: Damaged caused by
the explosion, taken between 1917 and 1918. The school was located at the
northeast corner of Albro Lake Road and Windmill Road.
Link: https://commons.wikimedia.org/wiki/File:Damage_to_
Tufts_Cove_School_after_Halifax_Explosion,_Tufts_Cove,_
Dartmouth,_Nova_Scotia,_Canada,_1917-1918.jpg

Back: House damaged by the Halifax Explosion
Link: https://commons.wikimedia.org/wiki/File:Halifax_
Explosion_Aftermath_LOC_1_-_retouched.jpg

Quarter Castle Publishing bore the complete cost of publishing this book and received no financial assistance from outside sources.

Quarter Castle Publishing
1787 Highway 2
Milford, Nova Scotia
Canada B0N 1Y0

0117QCP0021

Table of Contents

Halifax Explosion

The Halifax Explosion was the result of the SS *Imo*, a Norwegian vessel, colliding with the SS *Mont-Blanc* , a French cargo ship, in the Narrows of the Halifax Harbour on the morning of Thursday December 6, 1917, eleven months before the end of the First World War. The *Mont-Blanc* was carrying highly explosive picric acid, benzol, TNT and gun cotton.

The exact number of dead and injured people in Dartmouth and Halifax is unknown. The cities bustled with wartime activity, and many people passed through, heading to one destination or another. It is impossible to know if all bodies were recovered or counted. In one interview from 1957, a man who helped make grave markers said more than 3,000 were needed.

The confirmed deaths were 1,950. There were approximate 9,000 non-fatal injuries. More than 25,000 people were left homeless.

A more thorough history of the Explosion is found on page 147.

Blue

Sheila McDougall

HIS EYES WERE AS BLUE as the May forget-me-nots on Citadel Hill where they first picnicked on the cool spring earth. As blue as the cornflowers Mother grew in her summer garden. As blue as the harbour below, reflecting the summer sky.

When she'd go on, he'd colour up and shake his head in protest. "Don't be daft," he'd scold, but she could tell he liked it.

He liked her, too, more than her friends Jane and Mary who accompanied her to the waterfront that day. His cheeky compliments, spoken in accented English foreign to her ears, told her so.

He was short, not much taller than Kate, and slight of build. He looked no more than a boy, a handsome youth in his middy and seaman's cap, but his wit set him apart from the other young men jostling for notice.

Kate was where her parents had specifically told her not to be on the early spring day when she first met Able Seaman Mick MacIntyre. They had cautioned her to steer clear of the sailors stationed in Halifax, the smart alecs who loitered on the waterfront in their off hours, awaiting word of when they would ship out to God-only-knew-where God-only-knew-when. They reserved their harshest rebukes for the Brits who had no long-term investment in Canada and who looked down their noses at "the colonies".

"A limey will use pretty words to get up your skirt," her father warned, "but once you're in the family way, he will ship out never to be seen again, and your mother and I will be left with another mouth to feed."

Kate was sick of her parents' nag and jabber, their cautions about staying "a good girl", and the war in general. Anger—or was it worry?—lined their faces. In any case, there were few light moments in their household.

Her 12-year-old brother moaned about food rationing. His sweet tooth longed for sugar and butter and the fresh-from-the-oven cinnamon rolls smeared with melted icing when he came in from the cold at the end of a school day. When he whined, their mother retorted, "Don't blame me; blame the war." She took his complaints personally, as if he was accusing her of keeping the best for herself. Kate was rarely hungry: butterflies of infatuation had stolen her appetite.

A more serious but seldom acknowledged worry lurked in the background—the dread of German invasion, of fierce soldiers in spiked helmets goose-stepping down the streets, up their stairs and into their Halifax home.

At 17 and nearly finished school, Kate craved fun and escape from the hard-luck talk of her parents and the threat of war on their doorstep. Although a good student, no one at home or school spoke much about her future, or any future, as if they feared there might not be one.

Mick made her laugh, he made her feel special and despite the gathering signs he would soon ship out, he somehow made her momentarily forget the war. Kate loved him, and she felt certain her parents would love him too if only they gave him a chance. That didn't seem likely, so once her confidence grew in the company of her friends, she began sneaking out to meet him, taking care not to come face-to-face with her father who worked as a longshoreman and whom she feared meeting as he strode uphill from work, exhausted and irritable.

As the days warmed and lengthened, she and Mick flouted the rules, lolling on the side of Citadel Hill, flirting and getting to know each other while watching the comings and goings on the busy harbour below.

Mick, never very serious in the company of others, occasionally opened up to Kate of his homesickness and his longing for family. His blue eyes welled, and her heart ached for him.

He would soon be called to active duty but in the meantime, there were absences for naval exercises when Kate sobbed silently into her pillow, afraid her parents might hear.

Their mutual dread of separation intensified their closeness and longing, and they clung to each other with a sort of desperation. In the summer, they lingered on the Hill past dusk, inhaling the rich scent, a medley of salt air, warm earth and clover. Earlier, when there was more light, they searched for four leafs, omens of good fortune.

In the fading light, their embraces became more and more intense until one evening, Mick slipped a hand up her skirt to caress the soft skin above her stockings. Kate's heart raced and she felt breathless.

"Mick!" Her voice sounded thick and distant to her ears. She pushed him away and got awkwardly to her feet.

Both longing for and dreading a repeat of delicious but forbidden sensation, Kate tried to avoid spending too much time alone with Mick. Instead, they socialized with others and did their best not to dwell on his inevitable departure. Speaking of it would spoil what little time they had. Instead, they invented silly games and giggled at private jokes.

She'd cup his handsome face before they parted. "Oh-h-h, those eyes," she'd tease, and he'd shake his head and call her daft.

One day he took her closed hand in his and unfurled her fingers one-by-one. Then he gently shut her eyes with his fingertips.

She gave him a playful shove. "You'd better not be up to anything."

"Ssh, ssh," he whispered. And then she felt icy coldness on her palm. "Open."

"What's this?" In her hand lay two glass marbles.

"They're cat's eyes." He held one up to the waning light. "See? They're blue at the centre."

"Marbles. So I'm to take up children's games while you're

away?"

"No, no...Don't you see? They're blue at their centres. Like my eyes." He held each marble beside his eyes for comparison. "Cat's eyes are good luck."

"Oh, you silly bugger!" But she hugged him, and when he released her, there were tears on her cheeks.

"Now who's silly?" And he crushed her tears with his thumb.

As fall wore on and the sun set earlier and the weather grew colder, it became more difficult for Kate to account for absences from home. One evening when it was almost time to go their separate ways, Mick pulled Kate through the door of an outbuilding that housed a few horses. There was hay on the floor and bales stacked against a wall. Mick drew her to him and pulled her down.

The protective darkness, his soft kisses, the sweet scent of the hay and the sound of the horses' gentle breaths made her lightheaded.

They met there often that fall, and afterward she wondered if she was still a good girl.

~ ❧ ~

She had just left the house for school the day the world exploded. It was chilly that December morning, so she wore her warm jacket. In the right pocket were Mick's eyes. They were always with her, reminders of their love, even as his ship readied to sail out of Halifax Harbour.

Then she was lying on a cot surrounded by bustle and rush and moans of pain.

Someone took her hand, a big man judging by how his grip engulfed her small one. He identified himself as a chaplain and asked her name before telling her what she knew he had come to tell her.

A doctor examined her eyes and told her he must perform an enucleation. That meant he had to remove them because they had been shredded by flying shards of glass and could never be made to see again.

Kate had clung to her jacket after her rescue, refusing to

give it up despite its tears and smears of caked-on blood. She groped in the pockets until she heard the familiar clack of glass upon glass.

She held the marbles in her open palm and described how the blue of the cat's eyes matched the blue of her love's. She wished the doctor might somehow use them in place of her ruined ones.

But that, like her current reality, seemed far-fetched.

Sheila McDougall

Sheila McDougall is a former newspaper reporter, editor and freelance writer with several published short stories to her credit, one of which appeared in the Nimbus Publishing Ltd. anthology, *We Belong to the Sea*. She has also written a thriller, *City of Light and Shadow*.

Business as Usual

Phil Yeats

"JENKINS," MORROW, THE DUTY SERGEANT, called out as I followed two other patrolmen into the Halifax Police Station. "Get over here. Now!"

After finishing school in the spring of 1916, I'd volunteered for the army. I'd been declared unfit for service because of my poor vision and thrown back onto the streets, an outcast as I'd been through my school days. I'd always been excluded from sports and treated as an invalid because I wore spectacles.

Rejection by the army turned me into a different sort of pariah. Everyone saw me as a big, strong lad shirking my responsibility to fight the Hun. It didn't matter that I squinted at them through thick lenses and protested that I'd attempted to join the army. I was seen as a failure, a weak, passive coward who wouldn't fight for his country.

That fall, I joined the police force, thinking it was one way to do my patriotic duty and help protect the home front. The police wouldn't normally accept spectacles-wearing recruits, but they were short of men after the exodus of young constables to the army and navy. They accepted but didn't welcome me, and I joined patrolmen who were mostly too old for war service. Finally, in the days following the explosion of the French munitions ship SS *Mont-Blanc* on December sixth, 1917, I became part of the team.

"Yes, sir," I said as I turned towards the sergeant's desk.

Sergeant Morrow stared at the duty roster posted on the

wall beside him. "The police are no longer needed for rescue duty, and tomorrow is your day of rest. In recognition of the extra hours you've put in, I'm also giving you the rest of this day. Report for work at 0800 hours, Friday, when you will return to your normal schedule."

"Sir, does that mean we are no longer part of the rescue effort?"

"That's what I said, Jenkins. Friday you return to regular patrolman's duties."

After leaving the Duke Street station, I walked to Gottingen Street and headed for the centre of the Richmond district and the house where I rented a room. The explosion that had levelled more than a square mile of Richmond must have destroyed the house, but I hadn't been back since I left for work on the morning of the sixth.

On that first day, I spent eighteen hours digging victims from damaged buildings and sending them to hospitals or shelters. Facial injuries from shards of broken glass were the most distressing. Hundreds of victims were blinded or suffered from other problems that were far worse than mine.

That night, I'd snatched a few hours sleep at my sister's house south of Citadel Hill. The hill had protected her home from the worst of the blast, but many windows had been blown out and the front door had shattered. I returned to her house and helped with emergency repairs during the few free hours I'd had during the days after the explosion.

Now, I could anticipate a whole day for more robust repairs to her windows and doors. But first, I had to see what remained of the house I'd called home for the past year.

I walked north along Gottingen Street feeling sorry for myself. For one week, I had a real sense of purpose. The rescue work I'd done alongside city police and firemen, soldiers from the garrison, and sailors from the British warships had been crucial. No one looked at my thick lenses and suggested I should not be part of the effort. But when we return to normal activities, everyone from my colleagues to the sergeant and the public would once again notice my spectacles and suggest I was incapable of fulfilling a patrolman's duties.

As I approached my rooming house, the level of destruction increased. I realised my complaints were trivial compared to those of my landlady. She'd lost both her husband and her house, and for all I knew, her own life and the lives of her children. Her husband, like my sister's, enlisted after war had been declared. He'd been killed in France only months after he arrived overseas, leaving her alone with responsibility for two young boys. She'd rented the three upstairs bedrooms to single men such as me and dedicated the downstairs sitting and dining rooms for her boarders' use. She and the children occupied the kitchen and a windowless room that was little more than a pantry.

I found the house in the desolate landscape that had once been Richmond. Only the stone foundation and two short sections of wall in the corner with the room off the kitchen remained. Could those partitions have protected my landlady and her boys from the explosion's initial blast?

The late afternoon sun disappeared over the hills behind Fairview as I stared at the remains of the house. I turned and headed downhill towards Barrington Street and the harbour. In the fading light, the wreck of the steamship *Imo* was visible against the Dartmouth shoreline. What caught my attention, however, was a man on the Halifax foreshore almost directly in front of me. I proceeded down the hill until I came to a gully carved by a creek draining runoff water.

I unclipped the spyglass attached to my belt like an extra truncheon and hunkered down in the gully where I wouldn't be seen. The extra lens helped compensate for my poor vision.

As I watched the stranger pace back and forth with his gaze fixed on the water, I realised he had two companions. They were focussed on a large device, something resembling a bilge pump from an old schooner.

The larger man operating the pump was Herman Weber, a great brute not known for his intellectual capacity. He was usually seen in the company of James Bug-Eye Jones, a small-time crook and con man with protruding eyes. Herman's companion was shorter and of slight build but he was standing in a shadow, so I couldn't identify him. The stranger called out, and the two at the pump turned towards him. I got a good view of the third man; he was definitely Bug-Eye.

A stranger on the waterfront near the site of the previous week's explosion suggested something subversive, but Bug-Eye and Herman suggested more mundane criminal activity. Either way, I needed to report the situation. I abandoned my observation post and hurried along Barrington to the Duke Street Police Station.

"Jenkins," Sergeant Morrow bellowed when I entered the station. "Didn't I tell you to take the rest of the day?"

"Yes, sir, and I did. I was on my way home when I observed something I thought I should report."

"And what did you *observe*?" The tone of his voice suggested he would take nothing I said seriously.

A detective walking by paused as I related my observations to the sergeant. He left without saying anything but returned with a photograph.

"Is this the man?"

"Could be," I replied, as Sergeant Morrow turned away shaking his head. He didn't think I possessed any useful observational ability and never failed to remind me of his opinion. "It was almost dark and hard to identify his facial features," I said. "He was lean like this person and only a few inches taller than Bug-Eye, not nearly as large as Herman."

"James Jones is a scrawny little reprobate, only five foot two or three," the sergeant added. "Herman Weber is over six feet and two hundred pounds."

I pointed at the photograph. "He's nattily dressed, like the one in the photograph. Who is he?"

"William Slack. There's a warrant for his arrest in Montreal, and we learned he arrived here the day before the explosion."

"Well," I added. "The man on the foreshore could be this William Slack." I expected a blast from the sergeant for my interjections, but the detective rescued me by turning on Morrow.

"We should investigate. Round up some men, and Patrolman

Jenkins can lead us to the site."

Half an hour later, Detective Connors, five patrolmen and I arrived at the gully. The scene was unchanged. Herman continued to pump, Bug-Eye stood nearby doing something with a long hose, and the stranger stared across the harbour toward the *Imo*. I passed my spyglass to the detective, and he observed the goings-on without comment for several minutes.

"I'm convinced that's Bill Slack," Detective Connors said when the man on the foreshore turned towards Herman and Bug-Eye and exhorted them to work harder. "He's focussed on a float part way across the harbour," he added. "We should maintain surveillance until we know what they're up to. Then we arrest all three."

Later, the water roiled and a fourth figure emerged from beneath the waves. He was wearing a bulky suit with headgear and a contraption strapped to his back. When he reached the shore, the detective rushed forward.

"Move," he yelled. "You know your targets."

I followed Patrolman Burgess, one of the oldest patrolmen and a long-standing member of the constabulary who knew his job. He veered to the right to intercept Bug-Eye Jones, the only target that bolted. When Burgess blocked his escape route, Bug-Eye turned towards me.

I felled the diminutive Bug-Eye with a clumsy rugby tackle. The sports master at my school would have been disgusted with my poor technique, but my effort, more of a rolling block than a tackle, knocked Bug-Eye to the ground. After Burgess restrained him, I rushed to help the lone patrolman guarding the diver. He'd removed his helmet and the contraption I later learned was a re-breathing apparatus. His bulky suit was presumably intended to keep him warm in the frigid harbour waters, but he looked incredibly cold.

A few minutes later, Detective Connors had his four captives restrained, and his team prepared to escort them back to the station. I was free to resume my interrupted trip to my sister's flat but reluctant to abandon what had been my greatest adventure during my short tenure as a patrolman.

I spent my free day repairing my sister's second-floor apartment. I acquired wood to repair her front door but couldn't locate glass to replace broken windows. We, like hundreds of others, were reduced to tacking tar paper across the frames. Tar paper made an imperfect repair that didn't protect the rooms from winter's cold winds and had the disadvantage of being impervious to light. But we weren't as badly off as many others. Many windows had shattered but not all, so we still had natural light in several rooms.

Friday, I returned to routine patrolman's duties. The effort to rescue people trapped by the explosion that levelled the Richmond district had ended, and the long task of providing for injured and displaced people, initiated. Volunteers and supplies for the work were arriving from across Canada and the New England states.

That afternoon, I sat at a desk redrafting the illegible hands and almost incoherent prose of the patrolmen's daily reports. Other desk sergeants relied on verbal reports from the patrolmen, but Sergeant Morrow insisted on written ones. Many patrolmen were barely literate, and the sergeant had me rewrite their reports before leaving the station at the end of my shift.

I was hurrying through the unwelcome task when Detective Connor pulled up a chair.

"You should look at this." He placed a pamphlet—six or eight pages of typed text stapled together along the left-hand side—on the desk. "It describes exercises that will cure myopia. Sufferers who employ these techniques find they no longer need eyeglasses."

I shook my head. "Nothing will fix my vision."

"Perhaps not, but it could be improved. The exercises were designed by a physician named William Bates and I can assure you, his techniques work."

"And how do you know? This looks like a miracle cure con artists such as Bug-Eye Jones would sell along with a mystery potion."

Detective Connor pulled a pair of spectacles from a shirt

pocket. "Because I also needed eyeglasses but after employing Dr. Bates' *techniques*, my vision improved dramatically. Now, I only need my glasses when I'm overly tired. You should try."

"All right," I said as I folded the pamphlet and placed it in a tunic pocket. I wasn't convinced but in no position to question the veracity of the detective's claim. "What about Bug-Eye and the others? Have you discovered what they were doing?"

"They were attempting to collect a box of gold coins that was reputedly dropped off the stern of the *Imo* before she was abandoned."

"You mean by that man with the diving suit walking across the harbour from the Halifax foreshore. That's not possible. It must be five hundred yards to the *Imo*."

"I agree. It sounds far-fetched, and they didn't succeed. The diver had abandoned his attempt and returned to the Halifax side when we apprehended them. He had air supplied by both the pump Herman Weber diligently operated and a re-breathing apparatus that would supply him with air for thirty minutes. It could have worked, but he got off track and lost his sense of direction."

"Why wouldn't they approach the ship from the opposite side? The *Imo* can't be more than fifty yards from the Dartmouth shore."

"They would have been seen if they based themselves in Dartmouth. The plan depended on the devastation on this side of the harbour, and the fact it is virtually deserted."

"And the gold coins? Did someone really drop a box of coins off the ship?"

Detective Connor laughed and shook his head. "How old are you? Twenty?"

"Nineteen, but I will be twenty next month."

"Well then, young fellow, you have several lessons to learn from this experience. First, whenever something as monumental as this explosion happens, someone will sit in a tavern spreading wild tales of missing treasure."

"And the second?"

"It will be business as usual for the criminal elements. Con artists such as Bug-Eye Jones will search for opportunities to make a quick buck."

"And that's what happened here?"

"There were rumours before the explosion that someone on the *Imo* was smuggling gold and jewellery. We suspect Bill Slack was in Halifax with a scheme to acquire that gold. The explosion altered his plans, but he was still after it."

"But does it exist? And who's to say it wasn't offloaded from the ship and taken to safety by train?"

"People associated with the *Imo* and the Belgian Relief Commission deny there was any gold but rumours persist. That's all men such as Bill Slack and Bug-Eye Jones need to generate schemes like the one we defeated two nights ago. That, my young friend, will be our task for the months ahead. As the city rebuilds, Bug-Eye Jones and other criminal elements will devise new schemes to divert the relief money flowing into the city. It will be our job to stop them."

"Good luck with it. The rest of the patrolmen and I are back to our regular tasks of sorting out domestic disputes and the inevitable altercations in the taverns—and keeping the trollops in their place."

"That brings me to the purpose of this afternoon's visit. Two constables will be assigned to a team fighting corruption during the rebuilding of the city. I want you to be one of them."

～ ⚛ ～

Years later, I sipped wine as the police chief waxed poetic about the enlightened attitudes that allowed a nearsighted patrolman with little formal education to become Head of Detectives. It was 1961, and we were celebrating my retirement after forty-five years of service. I'd been daydreaming about my experiences during my first year as the chief droned on.

I would soon have to stand and make a speech. Should I describe how one broad-minded detective's attitude towards eyeglasses and a chance observation of clandestine activity allowed me to escape the drudgery of patrolman's duties?

In 1917, no one shared Detective Connor's enlightened attitude towards eyeglasses. Without his intervention, my police career would have ended when soldiers returning after the armistice in November 1918 replaced temporary patrolmen, especially nearsighted ones.

I decided to focus on the bizarre exploits of crooks trying to walk across the bottom of the Halifax Narrows and loot the SS *Imo*. I wouldn't criticize negative attitudes I encountered during my early years.

"There have been many changes since I joined the force during the First World War," I said as I summed up my remarks after relating my Halifax Explosion story. "Much more diversity and many new techniques but in the end, I have to return to my original mentor, Detective Michael Connors. He taught me that observation and logic were the heart of any investigation."

I removed my glasses and rubbed my eyes with the palms of my hands. "That gets me to my final thought. Detective Connor was a believer in new ideas and new techniques, but those newfangled ideas didn't always work. One example is particularly important to me. Mike advocated Dr. William Bates' regime of exercises that would cure myopia and obviate the need for glasses. He encouraged me to apply Dr. Bates' cure, but I have to say that was one of Mike's bright new ideas that didn't work."

I placed my glasses on my face and scanned the crowd. "To sum up, we need to be open to new ideas, new techniques and diversity of all kinds, but those have not changed the detective's primary focus. Careful observation and logical deduction are, and will always be, the basis for criminal investigation."

"And the gold?" someone asked from the back of the hall.

"Never been found, and if anyone thinks it ever existed, I have this bridge I could sell you."

Phil Yeats

Phil Yeats is a retired scientist experimenting with creative writing. He has a keen interest in environmental science and dabbled in yachting and golf before turning to fiction. He is the author of a handful of short stories and one poem. Several of these have appeared in two anthologies released by Dartmouth's Evergreen Writers Group, the latest, *Off Highway*, in October 2017.

Phil is interested in both science fiction/dystopia and mystery genres. His current project is a mystery novel featuring a detective in a fictional town on Nova Scotia's South Shore. Visit https://alkemi47.blogspot.ca for information about his writing projects.

Silenced Memories

Lawren Snodgrass

THE WARM BREEZE RUSTLED THE LEAVES on the potato plants as Wilber Coulson pulled weeds with a long-handled hoe. The showers the evening before and the warm July day had made the pesky plants explode overnight. Although Mathilda planned to weed, he insisted she rest instead. In her condition, she needn't be in the sun working when he could tidy the garden after work. Their son Everett also helped with the chores while she recovered from the most recent bout of bronchitis. Doc Fraser left little doubt her illness would not clear unless she rested and avoided her womanly chores.

Wilber paused for a moment, wiped his brow and leant onto the hoe to stare off at the harbour a few miles away. From his vantage point on Break Heart Hill, he could see the growing cities of Dartmouth and Halifax, their streets divided by the deep body of water. From this distance, he could not make out people, but he knew they were there. Given the hour, most workers had gone home for the night, yet many remained on the docks, loading or unloading and tending to ships either bound for overseas or arriving from there. The war created traffic jams in the harbour he had not seen for more than twenty years.

The ferries between the cities carried all traffic that needed to pass from one shore to the other—trucks, carts pulled by horses or oxen and passengers—to avoid the long trip around the Bedford Basin. He watched the *Dartmouth* approach the dock on this side of the water, its stack pumping black steam into the almost clear mid-summer sky, and memories from last December drifted into his mind: the smoke, the terror in the passengers' eyes, the frantic actions of the ferry crew.

He had been waiting to make the crossing when he heard shouts and looked to see thick black smoke pouring from the *Governor Cornwallis* ferry. It was still quite a distance from the dock, and onlookers speculated about the cause and whether or not help would go out to the ship or the ship would put ashore for assistance. Wilbur's first concern was *Would it explode?* He recalled staring at the flames, unable to move or respond to questions. Once again, he was a fifteen-year-old boy shocked by terrible sights, sounds and smells and running for his life. The horrid taste of burnt oil resurfaced and sweat beaded on his forehead.

A sudden thud and cries for help jolted him from his nightmare, and he sprang into action as he had done in 1917. The *Governor Cornwallis* had docked. Passengers scrambled for shelter, and workers directed the trucks off the burning ship. Wilbur helped an elderly couple to safety, then returned to help a mother and her four children, then a wounded soldier on crutches who had returned from overseas only the week beforehand.

In short time, the more than 300 passengers and 20 motor vehicles were on solid ground, and the ship was towed to George's Island and left to burn. He cancelled his trip to Halifax and instead returned home to Mathilda. She had seen the smoke, knew he would be there and when she saw him coming up the hill, she raced to him, threw herself in his arms and wept. They clung to each other, each reliving silenced memories of the first day they had met, the day they saved each other from Hell.

Wilbur forced the memory from his mind and tried to focus on the garden, eradicating the weeds, so he could return to his wife's side and reassure her all would be well, but a familiar chill raced up his back, expanded at his neck and caused him to shiver. He gently rubbed the left side of his chin where an ageing scar grew deeper with the years, and he ran his tongue over his dry bottom lip. Snapping back to the scene before him, he thought of his sons, Stephen and Leonard, both serving with the West Nova Scotia Regiment. They had been overseas for more than three years fighting the bloody Germans as his father had done earlier in the century. He silently cursed the British for not finishing them off the first time instead of forcing more young men to endure the same hardships.

He bowed his head for a moment of reflection, thankful his sons did not suffer the same fate as his father—death in the muddy trenches of war—and silently prayed they would return from Europe safely now that Germany had surrendered for the second time in 27 years. Their last letters home were positive, sharing their joy of victory and their ambitions after their ultimate return to Canada. All would be well, he assured himself, and allowed his muscles to relax and a smile to grace his lips. Life had been kind to him though challenging.

His eyes surveyed his well-kept property with his modest home, and he imagined his wife, content and for the most part healthy. They had built a life together in spite of the hardships, in spite of the wars, the flu epidemic, the Depression and everyone and everything lost during those years. Life was finally becoming easy, becoming less worrisome.

A resounding boom echoed in the evening air and although the shock wave wasn't strong enough to knock Wilbur off his feet, he collapsed to the ground, hugging it tightly, waiting for debris to rain down upon him. He squeezed his eyes shut and the past flashed against the dark backdrop. Bodies were everywhere, their figures nulled by thick black smoke that aimed to erase them from existence. Hot, burning breath instantly replaced the cool December air. It scorched his throat and stung his eyes. He tripped over a dismembered horse and its rider and stumbled into the bleak landscape searching frantically for familiarity. Clawing his way over debris, he forced himself to run full speed to escape the death that stalked him. He stumbled, fell and landed near a pile of rubble. Preparing to rise, a faint voice called out to him, freezing him in his tracks. His eyes darted over the broken wood, bent nails and shattered glass, searching for the source. When he saw her, his heart leapt into his throat. Her green eyes peered out from the darkness, pleading for help.

For a long moment, he was frozen in place. His head told him to *run, save yourself*, but his heart held him firm. He could not abandon her, leave her to die here alone.

"Help me, please, sir." Her voice, though weak, was determined.

An inner energy propelled Wilbur into action. He jumped up and surveyed the area quickly. The mound of debris was not formidable, and he threw it aside with all his might. When he finally reached her and pulled her to her feet, he saw she was drenched in oil, dirt, dust and blood and nothing more. He whipped off his coat and slipped her arms inside. It was almost long enough to reach her knees.

A loud bang made him search the sky for more flying debris, but none came. He turned to the girl and said, "We must get away from here." She nodded, and he started to run but stopped when she didn't follow.

"My leg," she said. "I cannot put weight upon it."

He ran to her side, pulled her arm across his shoulder and encouraged her to walk. In bare feet, she could not go fast, but after removing a pair of boots from the body of a headless woman sprawled on the street, they moved quicker.

"Wilbur!"

His senses snapped into place.

"Wilbur!"

He gulped for breath and raised his head from the garden dirt to look around. It was Mathilda running from the house. He scrambled to his feet and caught her in his arms.

"An explosion," she cried. "In the harbour!"

He searched the horizon and found a huge mushroom cloud—similar to what he'd seen in 1917—hanging over the far end of the harbour, deep in the Bedford Basin. Sirens and whistles accosted his ears as activity in the harbour grew, ships both large and small suddenly thrown into action. Imagining Windmill Road as it wound along the shoreline, he tried to pinpoint the location of the explosion. He watched the flames shoot into the sky, and his mind leapt on one fatal site: Canadian

Forces Ammunition Depot.

"Wilbur, what is it?"

He looked down at his wife, her green eyes filled with the same fear he saw the first day they had met. The large scar etched from her left nostril to her ear lobe twisted in loose skin as her face contorted. There was only one thing to do: run. "It's the Bedford Magazine," he gasped. "Ammunition from the war." For weeks, he had seen and heard of the munition arriving from overseas. The war was over, and it needed to be disposed of, but...once again, the destruction of war had come to his shores. He looked at her feet; they were bare. "Grab a coat and your shoes," he ordered. "We have to go." He pulled her towards the house, but she needed no encouragement.

Once inside, Wilbur grabbed his wallet and their small savings from the sugar dish. The crunching sound beneath his feet made him look down. Glass. He glanced around quickly. The windows facing the explosion had been shattered, suffering the same fate as thousands of others many years ago but thankfully, his wife did not wear the repercussions this time. As he waited impatiently for her to buckle her shoes, he thought about his youngest son. Everett had gone to visit a friend at the bottom of the hill. He had to warn him, get him to safety.

Mathilda stood, grabbed his hand and pulled him from the house. She coughed and sputtered as they sprinted down the driveway.

"Easy, Mattie," he said. He tried to slow her pace, but her grip on his hand told him she was running to escape the past as much as she was running to escape the present danger. He saw small groups of people running up Break Heart Hill. Relief washed over him when he recognised his son as one of them.

"Everett!" cried Mathilda. "My prayers are answered." She waved him to follow her as she coughed several times.

Another explosion erupted, making everyone duck while they ran. Wilbur glanced back at the harbour and watched the smoke plume grow. One minor explosion after another created a fountain of fire, as if it were fireworks and not deadly shells. Was there enough ammunition to repeat the disaster of 1917?

He hoped not. Still, he ran towards Cole Harbour, helping his wife who tired and gasped for air.

"Here, Mother." Everett grabbed her free arm and supported her.

"We're almost there," Wilbur said. "We'll be safe once we start down the other side. The hill will protect us." He sent up a prayer. The Citadel had saved those in Halifax from severe injury and death, and he predicted—with good faith—Break Heart Hill would do the same. They'd take refuge in Cole Harbour, stay there until the fire was extinguished. His daughter Kathleen and her husband Samuel lived there with their two children. They'd be safe.

A third blast sent ripples over Wilbur's shirt and tousled his hair. Pressure grew in his chest and in spite of the clear summer sky, all he saw was darkness. He stumbled and fell onto the gravel, rolling over his shoulder and landing in a heap. Once again, the past invaded his senses, and the burnt oil licked at his lips. The flames engulfing the homes lining the Halifax street threatened to snatch him from the ground and hurl him into the ocean. He glanced up and saw a dark figure hanging from the electric lines. His heart beat faster, and he feared it would leap from his chest and race off without him. A feral dog ran past him, throwing off his balance. He stumbled, but the girl he had rescued from the rubble held him securely, and he regained his step.

"This way," she cried, pulling him onto an unfamiliar street.

Unsure of her advice, he searched the area desperately, hunting for the way out of the war-torn downtown. He bulked and his feet grew heavy, eventually slowing to a stop. The heat lashed out at his face, and he feared any movement would make it unleash its fury.

"Come on! We have to go!"

The muffled sound of yelling reached his ears, but he hesitated to find the source. The fire watched him and if he moved, it would capture him. Its flame wrapped around his arm and tried to pull him closer, but he braced himself and stood firm.

"Run or we'll die!"

The fire screamed, but he knew not to move. A scorching slap

21

to his cheek shot pain to his head, and he looked down at the girl with the green eyes.

"We have to go this way." She pulled his arm and beckoned him forward.

He allowed her to lead him through the thick clouds and onto the street that took them past the inferno. Minutes later, they emerged from the thickest of smoke, and he looked up to see the outline of the town clock in the distance. They struggled on, and dark figures turned to human form, all moving towards the Citadel. The weight of the girl from the rubble grew, and he watched her struggle to keep moving up hill. He gathered his strength and with a surge of energy, he scooped her into his arms and carried her. She clung to him, sobbing quietly against his neck. They reached the far side of the hill where exhaustion brought him to his knees. They stumbled to a rock wall and flopped onto the cold, hard ground.

Wilbur felt a sudden tug on his arm and a strong set of hands lifting him off the ground.

"Father, we have to keep going."

He opened his eyes and saw his son's taunt face in his.

"Wilbur, it's not far now." Mathilda gripped his hand. "We'll make it, dear. Just a wee bit more to go."

He nodded, and once again, he supported the green-eyed girl over the crest of the hill and safely to the other side. The farms of Cole Harbour were a welcomed sight, and with the harbour falling out of view, his energy returned. When his wife stumbled, he paused, scooped her into his arms and continued onward. She clung to him, her eyes wet with fear.

By the time they reached Kathleen's home, Wilbur was exhausted. His son-in-law Samuel braced him and eased Mathilda onto the ground. They stumbled inside the farmhouse and collapsed into chairs.

"It's the Magazine," Kathleen said in a high-pitched voice. She dabbed a damp cloth on her mother's forehead. "Samuel's brother telephoned. He's at Rockingham and has a clear view of the explosions." She gulped for air. "I told him to run, to get as far away from there as quickly as he could."

Wilbur rubbed his face with his rough hands, leaving dirt and sweat behind. He and Mathilda had warned their children all their lives about explosions in the harbour. They had orders to run if a large fire threatened to become more than a house fire; it was more important to be vigilant during wartime when the dangers of enemy and friendly fire threatened their lives. A warm hand reached out and grasped his, and he looked to find the green eyes of an angel staring back at him, reassuring him as she had done many times over the years that everything would be okay. He conceded it would with her by his side.

Lawren Snodgrass

Born on an island at the edge of the Atlantic Ocean, Lawren Snodgrass learned how to swim quickly. His greatest fear used to be tidal waves; now it is not finding the time to put stories into words. His love of dime-store novels his grandfather shared with him ignited a love for westerns and the conception of the *Black Kettle Creek* western series.

Snodgrass is hard at work on the first book, *First Light of Death*, so don't expect him to show up to your dinner party.

Cellars and Sauerkraut

Catherine A. MacKenzie

NED'S STOMACH GROWLED. HE'D BEEN in a rush to leave home this morning and neglected to eat breakfast, and now he looked forward to dinner. His dear, sweet Maddie had promised his favourite meal of sauerkraut and pork chops.

His lids threatened to close, but he forced himself to stay awake. Thanks to their daughter Charlotte, neither Maddie nor he had slept the previous night, but who could fault a sick baby?

He stared at his to-do list and glanced at the calendar: December 6. He had to prepare a report on enrollment for the last three years. Though it was too early to finish the statement for 1917, he could work on the previous years, which necessitated descending to the dungeons of hell, as he referred to the basement, to retrieve data for 1915 and 1916.

"Okay," he muttered. If he sat at his desk much longer, he'd fall asleep for sure.

In the basement, he lingered too long reading documents from numerous boxes. Boring stuff, most of it, but other information, such as from where students hailed and their backgrounds, interested him. He'd read anything to avoid returning to his desk where sleep would surely befall him.

He sighed. He preferred completing work in a timely fashion rather than procrastinating. He replaced the papers where he'd found them, collected the stack of documents he'd gathered for the report and headed to the stairs.

Maddie wrapped the blanket around her daughter Charlotte, who was sick with fever. "Sleep, my baby, sleep." The four-month old had been awake most of the night, and Maddie hadn't slept. With Christmas three weeks away, she needed to complete the ribbing on Ned's socks and the tatting on Charlotte's dress. Thankfully, she'd finished the other Christmas gifts while she was pregnant and needed only to wrap them.

She peered out the kitchen window. Where were the signs of red Elsie Evans had predicted? Though the temperature had hit freezing overnight, the early morning was calm and clear, and the sun announced a wonderful day. There was no inkling of red that Maddie could see. She had scanned the sky the prior evening before going to bed. No red then either.

Maddie had conversed with Elsie the previous day while shopping at Lily's Grocery. Elsie, a deeply religious woman full of continual doom and gloom, warned of impending bad weather.

The elderly woman had wrung her hands and spouted, "Jesus said, 'When in evening, ye say, it will be fair weather: for the sky is red. And in the morning, it will be foul weather today: for the sky is red and lowering.'"

Though the parishioners of St. Paul's Church, including Maddie, were in awe of Elsie's scripture quoting, many believed the woman was crazy. Who but God could forecast the weather? Elsie was correct fifty percent of the time but with those odds, anyone could claim to be a weather forecaster.

Maddie turned from the window. She sat in her grandmother's rocking chair with Charlotte on her lap and caressed her baby's forehead. The fever was abating. "Sleep, my little one, sleep," she cooed. She kissed her forehead and rocked contentedly, happy the baby was improving.

Maddie felt bad Ned hadn't slept well the previous night. Though he'd gotten up late, he'd ensured the kitchen brimmed with warmth before he left for work. He hadn't had time for breakfast and would welcome pork chops and sauerkraut for dinner. She'd recently made her first batch of sauerkraut, thanks

25

to her mother's instructions. The only proper way to make the dish was to let the shredded raw cabbage and salt ferment in barrels for at least a month. *And no peeking*, her mother had admonished her. But Maddie couldn't resist sneaking several quick ganders.

She glanced at the clock: two minutes after nine. She eyed the knitting needles and grey yarn in the basket on the floor. Charlotte's eyelids fluttered. She thought it safe to lay her down, but when she placed her in the cradle, Charlotte's eyes popped open and she wailed.

Maddie sighed. It'd be impossible to finish Ned's socks with a fussy baby on her lap.

"Okay, let's get the sauerkraut. You and me." She'd figure out later how to carry a baby, a light and a pail of sauerkraut up the stairs but at the very least, she could check on the mixture. She lit the lantern, scooped up the baby and headed to the exit off the kitchen. As soon as she opened the door, the cave-like conditions of the cellar lambasted her. Gripping the lantern in one hand and Charlotte in the other, she descended the steep stairs. When she reached the damp dirt floor, she adjusted Charlotte and ambled to the other side of the room.

She was half way to the barrels when a humongous blast boomed overhead. Clatters, bangs, thumps and a mishmash of indistinguishable noises unlike anything she'd heard resonated from above. The lantern slipped from her fingers, the flame extinguishing when it hit the floor. Her arm instinctively tightened around Charlotte, who wailed and squirmed.

"Sssh," she mumbled.

The dark. Oh, the dark.

What happened? Earthquake? She was positive the ground shuddered and the foundation's walls swayed before she dropped the lantern. Would the house collapse?

She felt debris swirl around her face and settle on her skin. Timbers above her rumbled and groaned. She covered Charlotte's head with her arm and tucked her close to her breast.

She didn't know what to do. She couldn't remain in the cellar yet the upstairs might be unsafe. Peering through the darkness, she strained to see the stairway.

She stood for several long moments while Charlotte bellowed. The air became thick, and Maddie gasped for breath. With her right hand, she groped along the wall, manoeuvred around junk, touching sharp chunks of concrete and hoping to avoid creepy crawlers and spider webs.

She inhaled, needing to breathe but abhorring the intensified odours that invaded her nostrils—mildew, mustiness, mould—and the riled-up dust that clogged her air passages and stuck in her throat. She sneezed.

Her foot hit a solid object. Feeling around in the dark with her free hand, she found it to be the stairs. She switched Charlotte to her right shoulder, grasped the railing and stepped onto the bottom step.

She made it to the top tread and pushed against the door. When it slid open, the draft and the eerie quiet assaulted her. Light from the broken windows highlighted floating dust particles.

Pots, pans and framed photographs had fallen from hooks on the wall. Broken dishes and glassware lay strewn about the room. Worst of all, the china closet had toppled, splintering her late grandmother's rocker. Her work basket and the baby's cradle had disappeared in the rubble.

Her eyes welled. "My goodness!" She gripped Charlotte and lowered her face to her baby, inhaling the still-present newborn fragrance. "Your cradle. You were just there. So was I."

Carefully stepping over debris, Maddie reached the window. Puffs of white smoke rose in the distance near the harbour.

Her heart skipped a beat. "Ned!" She leant against the wall. She couldn't pass out, not holding Charlotte. She had to remain strong. For her baby.

But Ned!

Ned worked downtown at the Royal Naval College of Canada in the north end of the HMC Dockyard. By the harbour!

~ ❧ ~

Ned stirred and opened his eyes. Indescribable agony wracked his body. He had difficulty swallowing. His mouth felt stuffed with cotton, and his dry tongue touched a gritty film on his lips. His nose itched, but he couldn't move his arms to reach his face.

He tried to remember what had happened and where he was. Anything. Something.

He had gone to the basement. For papers. What happened after that?

He stared at joists above him. He was still in the basement, lying on the floor, covered in rubble and debris. Rumbling echoed in the distance, and odd noises reverberated throughout the building. Thankfully he could wiggle his toes and move his legs.

Maddie!

He shoved off wreckage and managed to stand. Shooting pains coursed through his back. Blood dotted his hands. He stumbled over debris, carefully avoiding glass shards, jagged metal and broken bricks. The stairs were intact.

He had to get outside.

He reached the first floor and gasped. Part of the north wall had crumbled, leaving a gaping hole to the outdoors. He peeked into his office. Timbers and plaster covered his desk. Papers, bricks and wood planks riddled the room. He had to get out while he was still alive.

The Germans! They'd finally done it. Hadn't he heard the planes, that faint roar while in the basement? He shook his head; nothing could be heard when in the dungeon. But what then?

The Great War had raged overseas for three and a half long years. The war finally hit home, and the Germans had dropped a bomb—or bombs—on the seafaring port of Halifax. He'd feared an attack for months and was surprised it had taken this long. Since the war had started, the harbour bustled with troops and ships, along with shipments of war supplies. Halifax had been founded in 1749—Ned fancied historical facts—as a military outpost of the British Empire and once the city became known as an international port and naval facility, it was placed on the map. This activity left it wide open for a German attack.

What was left of his city? And what about Maddie and Charlotte? His stomach knotted. He flexed his fingers, ready to

28

take on whatever came his way.

The outdoors was shrouded in fog, grey and dull as if dark glasses obscured colour. He rubbed his eyes to clear his vision and regretted it immediately, for gritty bits scratched his eyeballs. He wiped blood-smeared fingers over his sooty pants.

He scanned the carnage from outside the college building. The structure was once the former naval hospital, built in 1863 to replace the original hospital that had been destroyed in the 1815 fire. It was later refurbished to house the college. The structure would again have to be rebuilt or torn down.

Other than fireballs shooting over the harbour and faint, indistinct echoes in the distance, the area was deserted. Was he the only survivor?

His paternal grandfather had relayed stories of the Crimean War, and the destruction facing Ned was how the younger Ned envisioned a war-torn city. His ears ached and he feared he had been deafened in the blast. The city was too silent.

Seconds later his ears buzzed and smells assaulted his nostrils. His nose itched, but he didn't dare touch his face again. He knew without looking it had been lacerated, and drops of blood plopping on his sleeve confirmed this.

He proceeded away from the harbour towards home, covering his head with his bloody hands as he went, unsure of the streets he encountered. Barrington, Duke.

Duke? The street didn't look like Duke and neither had Barrington resembled Barrington Street. The farther he walked, the more alive the streets became—no, not alive, less dead. Unrecognizable streets ablaze with bonfires and mayhem confronted him no matter where he turned. Clouds of smoke buffeted into the sky. Trees had been snapped in half, and numerous branches had been tossed about. Crippled metal and white-hot shards of iron littered the ground. Buildings, indistinguishable from their former states, had collapsed.

Individuals shrieked and howled as banshees or were quiet as spies sworn to secrecy. Men either darted by, heedless of what might be underfoot, or ambled, expressionless, disbelieving of the chaos. Wide-eyed women in torn dresses and missing shoes staggered about senselessly.

He reached Gottingen Street quicker than he had anticipated and gawked at The School for the Deaf. Other than shattered windows, the building appeared intact. Oh, those poor, petrified children. Perhaps it was a blessing in disguise they couldn't hear; maybe they'd missed the commotion. He listened closely and was positive he detected hollow screams, evidence confusion had entered the children's dark worlds. He shook his head. No, he couldn't hear them; the massive brick building was silent save for nearby guttural noises.

Several people wandered past aimlessly, stumbling as if blind. The Halifax School for the Blind on Morris Street wasn't in his direction, so he tried to shake the images from his mind. To be unable to see, unable to know what had happened and unable to fathom what would occur next would be horrible.

Guilt washed over him when he eyed the School for the Deaf again. Or had it viewed him? Could buildings become animate? He should lend assistance—no, he had his own child to think about.

He scooted by as quickly as he could, pretending he hadn't seen the building looming before him.

And then it hit him. He'd deserted the college. He shouldn't have left before checking on his coworkers and the students. His saving grace—if he had one—was he'd been in the basement when the attack occurred, but others wouldn't have fared as well. He couldn't have searched all three floors himself. He couldn't save everyone. His family depended upon him.

Suddenly chilled by the frosty December weather, he shoved his hands into the pockets of his thin sweater. Structures burnt alongside him and he could have warmed himself by walking closer, but it would be sacrilegious to take comfort from another's loss. He hesitated, watching smoke gush from windows of a once-stately house. Within minutes, the sagging roof plunged and disappeared. His stomach lurched. How had his house fared?

He passed an obese woman with long, deep gashes on her exposed flesh. Heavy breasts drooped to the waistband of her rumpled skirt. Minutes later, he met another woman. Her left eyeball dangled upon her cheek, held by a mere filament.

A voice shouted, "What's happening?"

No one answered or if they did, Ned didn't hear because he continued to walk towards home.

He glimpsed flecks of colour amongst the colourless world and thought his eyesight was recovering: bright reds, dull reds, pinks. Blood, he thought, then saw bits of blues and greens amid the rubble.

The stink of burning flesh permeated his nostrils. He'd never smelt such an odour. Once a person smelt death, they never got over the stench. He held his breath and tried to not breathe deeply—at least not until he passed the atrocities, where he might then inhale a great gulp of fresh air. But when he thought he could take an unspoiled breath, none surfaced.

Nothing but ugliness, heinousness and dehumanization faced him.

A frantic young man, his face blackened and clothes tattered, gripped Ned's shoulders. He fought off the creature.

"Calm down," the stranger muttered. "Just trying to help."

Ned extricated himself from the strong hands and moved away. He didn't need help. He was fine. "I'm not like the rest of you," he screamed.

Minutes later, yearning to talk to someone—anyone—he latched onto an older man's arm. "Germans," he said, despite the man's vacant eyes. "The Germans have attacked."

But where were the planes he had heard?

Maddie! Charlotte! He'd dawdled. He had to keep going.

In his rush, he narrowly missed tramping over a headless body and when he looked up, he saw two individuals draped over telegraph wires. He saw images of those in worse condition. The dead hung from smashed windows. They appeared curious as if they'd been stretching as far as they could to look down the street and then gave up. Others stood silent, peering from blackened windows and doorframes. He assumed many others were trapped in homes, for he had passed entire blocks caught up in infernos.

Bile rose, and he bent to release it. With the edge of his sleeve, he wiped his face. He glimpsed an individual in stark contrast to previous impaired women: heavily made up, flowing gown, high heels. A lady of the night? Though appearing unharmed, she mumbled and moaned. Mental, he figured. She'd gone crazy. But hadn't he, too? The world had gone crazy.

He felt numb and only his quivering legs worked, moving him forward. Germans, their burnished helmets perched on top of their heads, could appear at any moment from around a burning building or out of a wreckage heap.

Had he missed them—the Germans? He'd averted his eyes more than once, even walking with his head down at times, so he wouldn't know what lay either side of him. He watched only where he placed his next step.

But no, the enemy would have made their move, would have announced their presence with gunshots or more bombs. He admonished himself to be more aware—unless...Had he been mistaken? But if not the Germans, who? Was there another evil force at work? His cynical father had proclaimed the world's demise many times. Had that time arrived?

He shuddered and almost stepped on a rotten log. No, a leg. Charred. Other limbs and bodies burnt beyond recognition presented themselves. He could not identify them and knew not if one belonged to a friend. At one point, he clamoured over several mangled bodies in order to avoid burning rubble. There was nowhere else to go. He didn't want to veer from the road. The Germans might be waiting.

He reached Northwood Street. A man appeared out of nowhere and walked in his direction.

"Harbour's on fire!" the stranger shouted. "Ships exploded."

Ned gripped his arm. "Slow down. What you say?"

The distraught man wriggled from his grasp and pointed behind him. "Fire. In the harbour."

"Germans." Ned remembered when a German U-boat had torpedoed the Canadian hospital ship HMHS *Llandovery Castle* in June. Despite the incident taking place off southern Ireland, it was one of the worst atrocities to hit Canada. And now this!

"No, two ships," the man said. "Collided. The *Mont-Blanc*."

The *Mont-Blanc*? Ned had walked along the harbour the previous morning when the French cargo ship, on her way to France from New York, steamed in. His eyes widened. "The *Mont-Blanc*?" Not the Germans?

"The *Mont-Blanc*, yes."

The ship carried military explosives, and Ned realised the seriousness of the situation and how lucky he'd fared. He could see, move his arms, walk. He mouthed a prayer. *Please, God, save us.*

Minutes later, he encountered Elsie Evans standing at what used to be the corner of Parker and Norward. "Elsie, you okay?"

Her dark eyes bore into his. "Told ya so. I warned Maddie yesterday. Did she tell ya? It'll be stormy tomorrow, I tells her. And see it today?" She pointed to the sky. "The sky's red and threatening." Weariness emanated from her as if she'd given up.

You're one of the lucky ones, he wanted to say. *You and I. We're alive.* But he didn't want to rehash the horrors if she questioned him, didn't want to waste time explaining about the ships. And what did he know anyhow?

"Mark my words." She waved her arms like a mad woman. "Blizzard a comin'."

"Keep safe, Elsie."

Finally, Albion Row was in his sight. Home! At first glance, the street appeared unscathed but as he neared, cracked and smashed windows confronted him. Several doors had been blown from doorframes, and trees bordering the street had been splintered. The brick buildings looked intact, but outward appearances were deceiving.

Syd, his and Maddie's landlord, sat on the stoop at number 89 Albion. Slivers of glass protruded from his face. One eye was bloodied. Ned comforted the old gent, who spoke incoherently. "You'll be okay," Ned said, rubbing the elderly man's arm. "Sit tight. I'll be back. I have to get Maddie."

Ned and Maddie's home was number 87; Syd lived in the

attached building. If Syd looked like that—

The sight of blood had never bothered him, but he'd seen too much. The group of frenzied, bloodied children who had raced with flailed arms flashed before him. Would Charlotte reach their age? He gagged several times, needing to rid himself of the horrific scourges he'd viewed and ingested, as well as the *every man for himself* attitude he'd adopted. How selfish of him!

But then Maddie, cradling Charlotte in her arms, appeared at the doorway.

"Maddie," he screeched, and they raced toward each other.

From the Author

This fictional story was inspired by a true story from my third cousin, Elizabeth Cardoza Taylor, who states: *My mother and grandmother were at home on Princess Place (just off the Common). My mother was sitting in a small wooden rocker in front of the china cabinet. My grandmother decided she needed sauerkraut from the barrel in the basement for the meal she was preparing for my grandfather—he was on military duty on McNabb's Island (I believe) but would be home later. My grandmother scooped up my mother and took her with her to retrieve the sauerkraut. The explosion happened while they were in the basement. When they eventually returned to the kitchen, the china cabinet had fallen over and crushed the chair my mother was sitting in. She always said her life was saved by sauerkraut, and that's why she loved it. The house had broken windows, but I don't think there was major damage. It was half of a double. A relative who lived in the other half had opened the sliding door into the parlour to clean. She was blown through the opening by the explosive force and would have been injured had she not opened the door earlier. The sauerkraut barrel in question was, I believe, in the basement of the other half of the house.*

Sadly, no one really talked to me about those times, particularly my grandfather who, I am sure, saw more than he wanted to remember. Some of the houses on Princess Place still exist (with historic plaques of some sort) but theirs does not.

Catherine A. MacKenzie

Catherine A. MacKenzie escapes from her mundane world by writing poems and short fiction most women can relate to. Although she writes all genres, she enjoys veering towards the dark. She has been published in many print and online publications. She has also self-published several short story collections, books of poetry and children's picture books.

Cathy lives with her husband in Halifax, NS. She and her husband usually winter in Ajijic, Mexico, where her works have appeared in local publications.

Her amazing, gorgeous grandchildren provide much of her joy and inspiration.

Visit Cathy's website at https://writingwicket.wordpress.com.

Ruins, Glass and the Opportunities They Present

Polly J. Brown

THE FARM BECKONED. AT FIRST, it whispered through the sweet scent of strawberries bathed in morning dew, then sang by crisp green grass glowing in sunlight moments after a rain shower. By the time the leaves had painted themselves into rusts, yellows and oranges, Henry couldn't ignore the cry to return home.

He sat on the edge of his bed and traced the bumps and creases of the paper with his thumb, floating over the words he didn't want to read. Weak. Sick. Letters, which spoke of missed plantings, lost livestock, collectors at the door. A wage of seventy cents per day from the city helped but couldn't replace an able body, especially when it belonged to the only son left.

Time had finally caught Henry, something it failed to do during the war, and he wasn't prepared. He had one more thing to do before returning to the family home and accepting the legacy his father was about to leave.

He set the letter on his bed and rubbed the remnants of a dream from his mind. Waves of honey-coloured wheat waiting to be harvested. Cows grazing in the opposite field. The sweetness of blueberry preserves spread over warm biscuits. He shook them away, unwilling to give in. Not yet. He needed one more day.

An early autumn breeze flickered through the crack in the window, planting goosebumps along the breadth of his arm, and he swiftly dressed in clean clothes before a chill set in. He took extra care while shaving the cleft in his chin, mumbling the words he longed to free, and slicked his brown hair so not one strand stood out of place. With a final look in the small square mirror on the wall, he was ready for the day, one which would send him home in either misery or elation.

Most occupants of the boarding house still slept but when he walked into the kitchen, Mrs. Young was clattering at the stove. She'd pinned her hair in the usual salt and pepper bun, and spots of flour sprinkled her black dress despite the apron she wore.

"Good Morning, Mr. Whitman," she said and placed a cup of tea in front of him.

"Good Morning. Thank you."

"It looks like rain today. You should take an extra sweater with you if you're working on the roofs."

Henry filled his plate with the bread and cheese laid out on the table. Yesterday's paper lay on the seat beside him, and he angled it to read the headlines.

The rustle against the wood was all Mrs. Young needed. "Some union members are threatening to strike again. Those poor families suffered enough, losing everything in the explosion. They shouldn't have to wait two years to have a home. It's time I wrote a letter to the reconstruction committee and gave them a piece of my mind. This nonsense is unacceptable." She tsked three times and turned her attention to the stove.

"I'm sure the others will be happy to tell you the details." The warm bread weighed heavy in his stomach. Strike. Another reason to leave. The rumblings and threats didn't capture Henry's support. Even the men who now flinched at the slightest bang of a hammer or squeal of a saw needed to earn a living. Heroics and laurels didn't pay rent. Too bad his fellow members didn't agree.

Mrs. Young stirred the pot. "No doubt they will. However, I'd prefer to hear your thoughts. You seldom speak your mind, but you're thinking. The quiet ones usually are."

Henry slurped his tea by accident. He covered his mouth with a hand as he set the cup down. "I think focussing on the task, rather than the hurricane surrounding them, is the smarter course of action."

His landlady smirked. "Just like waking up early while the bread's warm and there's plenty of tea. You have the most sense out of all my boarders. You shouldn't be fraternizing with that bunch." She raised her eyes to the floor above and as if on cue, the ceiling belched a muffled thud, followed in quick succession by several heartier ones.

"I don't fraternize," Henry said, plucking a bit more cheese and an apple for his plate. He listened for the footsteps on the stairs before lowering his voice to a hush. "I'm here for the work, not for friendship."

His landlady placed a bowl of porridge on the table. "Smart man. But you're here for more than work." A smile tiptoed across her lips. "Have you spoken to her yet?"

The plate rattled when Henry dropped the apple. "N-no. Today." He gulped, certain his nerves anchored in his throat. "On the way to work. I never faced anything like this during the war."

Mrs. Young lifted her eyebrows. "You'll do fine. Just remember the hints I gave you."

A rhythmic thump on the stairs ended the conversation. Henry ducked his head, focussing on the bowl in front of him rather than the three men entering the kitchen. Newer additions to the boarding house. Scruffy, unkempt loud talkers, who returned every evening smelling of ale and women. Over the past year, Henry had seen faces come and go, and he gave up learning names about six months in. These three needed to move along.

The porridge smelt of maple and burned his tongue.

"Porridge again," said the man with ink-black hair. His beard trailed to his chest and almost covered the stain on his shirt. He grabbed the chair closest to Mrs. Young and turned it around before sitting. "I pay for more than this."

Mrs. Young placed four more bowls at the table. "Mr. Wells, you pay for room and board. Meal offerings weren't specified." She returned to her busywork, ignoring the mutters of displeasure.

Henry rose, careful not to scrape the chair against the floor. With a nod of thanks, he retreated to his room and the small

38

square mirror to practice his speech one final time.

He'd hoped to avoid his house mates on the walk to work but moments after he set foot on the street, the door behind him slammed and natter replaced the morning silence.

"...need to go," one of the men said as they passed Henry. "Those jobs are for union men."

"There's talk of a strike," said another. "Meeting's taking place tonight."

"We should go," Wells said and turned to Henry. "You comin' with us?"

He shrugged. "I promised to help Mrs. Young repair a window. I'll be along after that." Unless he dragged out the window repair well into the night.

Wells shook his head and turned the corner, providing Henry with a moment's relief. Unions, strikes, more reasons to return to farm life. He'd squirreled enough money to keep life comfortable in difficult seasons and with his father's failing health, he had no reason to stay.

The city blossomed before him. Trees framed the streets in veils of orange, yellow and red, hinting of the harvest. Their whispers escorted him along streets lined with wooden homes, past the Citadel to the place where trees had snapped like matchsticks when the munitions ship exploded. Buildings popped up in rapid succession, but the north end neighbourhood didn't hold the same character as it had before the shock wave tore it apart. Stone replaced wood. New families replaced the dead.

Despite the new construction, the harbour view was unimpeded. Sparks of sunshine danced around boats on the water. Waves rippled like a field of wheat, and seagulls squawked overhead.

A twinge of doubt poked at his chest. He'd miss the water and the stream of cargo ships which sailed into port. But regret would pour in if he missed his opportunity. He had perhaps one chance left, and it couldn't be squandered.

It took eighteen hundred and sixty-seven steps from the boarding house to reach his favourite street. One hundred and fifty more to his favourite house. As he neared, his steps slowed.

He fixed his cap and straightened his back while ignoring the flush which grew on his cheeks. Sweaty palms brushed his thighs.

A few more steps. A few more moments.

She emerged from the side door with an armful of washing blocking her face from view. Henry didn't need to see it. He remembered every strand of her chestnut brown hair and how the curly tendrils escaped no matter how she pinned it. He knew every crease on her face when she smiled and every curve of her scar, the one that framed the right side of her face from temple to chin.

Ahead of him, Wells threw a look her way and laughed. "The old maid's busy at work again. I'll stop by for my drawers later, sweetheart." The group laughed and continued down the street.

Henry's fists clenched at his sides. The way Wells tormented her every morning disgusted him. That scar was fresh, tinged pinked and hadn't faded to a darker tone as most scars eventually did. Guessing when she'd gained it was easy, but Henry didn't want to know how many ghosts she'd seen in the process. Too many, he supposed.

He'd never asked. Twice a day for a year he passed her home. Tipped his hat. Smiled. Noted how her hands grew cracked and red when the leaves fell and the rain changed to snow. He'd even worked the courage to stop once to ask the price of laundering a shirt but the craggy, middle-aged woman answered the door instead, so questions went unspoken.

She paused for a moment as the workers strode past. Chin held high, she kept her battered face on display. The tight purse of her lips told Henry she'd heard them. When the raucous voices faded, she turned her face to the street.

He reached for the notes tucked in his pocket and gripped them tightly. Her entire face was visible; one side scarred and one side smooth. The milky eye on the right two shades of ocean blue lighter than the one on the left. Lips the deep pink of lady's slippers. Skin like the mayflowers dotting the woodlands behind the farm. It was the best part of his day for over a year though he had never found the courage to speak to her. Until today.

Henry stopped at the path to the door, smiled and tipped his hat as he had done each day before.

She stilled. The faded sheets in her arms softly rustled with the morning breeze, and her fingers curled into the fabric. The corner of her mouth flickered, and Henry thought a warm blush crept over her cheeks.

He gulped the tightness down his throat and inhaled a deep breath. When he approached by four more steps, the earth trembling beneath his feet, she took three down the stairs to the ground.

The shaking of his hand steadied as he removed his cap. "Good Morning, miss. My name is Henry Whitman."

Patience only went so far and Mabel's had thinned a season ago. She massaged salve into the crevices streaking once dainty hands. The sting was easy to ignore; it paled in comparison to glass slashing her skin. She perused the sea of clothing dotting the backyard from her bedroom window. With the soft west wind they billowed in waves, rising and falling like the tide in the harbour. Once a refuge and salvation, her small sea of cloth edged to the point of burden. It provided money, yes, but clogged Ivy's house and both it and she loomed at the point of annoyance.

Being a laundress was an unexpected turn of fortune. As a young lady, she'd knit a fantasy of what her life would be. The troop train would chug to the pier and a handsome soldier would declare himself before sending letters from an ocean away. Later, she'd spend her days as her mother had—rearing children, saying prayers, tending house. But prayers hadn't stopped the church from collapsing. Nor had it stopped the school from tumbling like a deck of cards. They certainly hadn't prevented the rain of glass. The explosion had shredded more than just her eye. Sometimes as she watched the flow of fabric and her thoughts drifted, she wondered if any part of the girl she was remained.

With a final sweep of a pin into her hair, she left the solace of her room and followed the trail of frustration to the kitchen. She loitered at the threshold and tucked out of sight when someone in the kitchen huffed.

"Everywhere!" Ivy, the wife of her father's foreman, threw her hands in the air and moved a basket near the side door. "There are times I would like our home back."

"I know, but the girl has nowhere else to go. Have pity," replied her husband, James.

A wave of sadness flooded Mabel. James had been at her side when she woke in the hospital and delivered the heartbreaking news about her family. She returned the gesture with gratitude, work and money, but pity only went so far. Ivy deserved her home restored; Mabel required one of her own. The reconstruction efforts stalled the possibility.

A heavy sigh fell from Ivy's lips. "I do, but I didn't see this continuing so long." Chair legs clattered against the wood floor.

"And she can't see at all," James replied. A newspaper snapped, then rustled when he turned the page.

Mabel pursed her lips until they were as thin as thread. Quite an exaggeration. One eye worked fine. A whiff of dust kissed her nose, and she coughed before entering the kitchen.

"Good morning," Ivy said and pointed to a basket on the floor. "These arrived for you from the lady a block down. The one with the rambunctious boy who climbed our tree last year."

Mabel eyed the basket and the four other piles scattered about the room. "Mrs. Wilson."

"Yes. She will fetch them tomorrow." Ivy smiled and sixty years of lines framed her eyes. "Come. Have some bread and butter before you start."

Mabel edged forward and slipped into the nearest chair. She inhaled the yeasty steam rising from the table and her stomach gurgled in delight.

James shook the paper again. "Union's talking of strike. That'll set the restoration back weeks, maybe months. Those neighbourhoods will never be finished at this rate, and mark my words those waiting for homes won't be pleased."

The knife glided across Mabel's bread, butter melting into every pocket. She chewed, allowing James's opinion to remain unchallenged. The wait for a home was a stain on filthy cloth, and the north end ceased being her neighbourhood the same instant her family perished. Ghosts of her siblings lingered on every corner, the memories bringing swift bouts of joy followed by pangs of sorrow. Halifax had become tarnished and dull.

The clock in the hall chimed quarter past seven and with each note, Mabel chewed faster. In three hundred seconds, the tradesmen would begin walking by. One hundred and fifty more before her favourite would pass.

He had kind eyes, brown like the soil in her mother's garden, and he kept his dark hair longer than most, even the random strands that hinted at years beyond his youth. His work clothes were without patches or tears, and he kept himself shaven every day without fail, keeping the cleft of his chin on display. Callouses adorned his hands and a jagged scar ran down one palm, the sole hint of the horrors contained in muddy walls.

Maybe today, instead of a stare and a blush, she would speak.

After a quick glance of the clock, with two hundred and twenty nine seconds remaining, she gulped her tea, swept her crumbs and gathered the newest pile of clothing into her arms before heading out the door. The autumn air met her as a crisp wall tinged with smoke and mulch. Wisps of her breath floated to the clouds, and her hands hurt. Nevertheless, the morning was lovely.

Until it wasn't. Men like Mr. Wells and the pack of workers striding by never stayed quiet. They unnecessarily filled space and shouted mindless opinions about the union with pride. She could've dropped her pile and retreated inside but didn't want to miss her favourite.

"I'll stop by for my drawers later, sweetheart." Mr. Wells made an obscene gesture with his hands, but his words nudged her like muffled cotton. If any blessing came from the day the city blew up, it was that she could turn a blind eye and a partially deaf ear, effectively shunning them from existence.

Fifteen seconds until they passed. She pursed her lips for ten. Changes in circumstance hadn't stolen her pride.

She turned when she reached the count of two, her favourite

one slowing his steps. When he neared the path, he smiled and tipped his hat as he had done every day before. And as she had done every day before, she smiled and struggled to contain the blush of her cheeks. But today he took four steps towards her, stumbling over a stone before righting himself. Her heart pattered with anticipation. Finally he had made a gesture. Finally, she would. She took the three steps to the ground and turned to study him with her good eye.

A small bead of sweat pooled at his temple; his hands wrung the cap they held. He breathed deeply, then spoke. "Good morning, miss. My name is Henry Whitman."

His voice reminded her of mellow butter and fresh spring days, and she closed her eyes, allowing the sound to sink into memory. The silence that followed caused her to snap them open again and the blush on her cheeks grew.

"Good Morning, Mr. Whitman. I am Mabel."

"Mabel," he repeated with a tense smile. "I wondered if I may have a moment of your time." His boot shuffled the gravel.

The tightness in her chest prevented anything other than a nod, even though she had a hundred questions ready to jump from her mouth.

He stared at his boots. "I'm working on the reconstruction, but my family lives on a farm in the valley. After the war, I came to Halifax to earn enough to help them. I'm the last son, you see." He toed a stone. "Father's getting weak and I must return. Every day I walk past and I've always meant to stop and say hello. Maybe get the courage to ask you to court. I shouldn't have waited." His gaze moved upwards, and he met her eyes with a slight hesitation. "I'm a hard worker. I will make you proud to have me."

"Have you?" She clutched the sheets tighter to her chest, constricting it from both the inside and out.

"Yes, I know it's sudden, but I'd like to have a wife. I'd like it to be you."

The wind rustled strands of hair across her face. Her grip on the sheets slackened. He was leaving the city. He wanted a wife. He proposed to a stranger. To her. Despite the scar that marred

44

her face and the blindness in her eye. The man must be insane. Perhaps a shell had exploded too close or the wait to return home had taken too long. Or maybe, his motives were cruel—to inflate her hopes for a normal life only to raze them until they crumbled to ash. But the sincere smile and hopeful glance made her stomach dance and the colour in her cheeks retreat.

"Come again?"

Henry removed another step between them. The furrow on his brow told her he hadn't caught the fire in her question. He wrung the life out of his hat.

"I'd like to,"—a deep breath—"have your hand. If you'll have me, of course. The farm is a good size and we have some cows, goats, chickens. There's a decent vegetable plot if you're interested, and we're not far from the river—"

"You're serious." The question fell to a statement as disbelief crept away.

Henry's confused expression morphed into certainty. "Why, yes. I know we don't know each other well. If I'd been courageous sooner, we would but don't let it distract you. I'll give you all the time you need and tell you anything you want to know. I'm not like them." He flicked a finger towards the absent workers. "I know about losing loved ones. My home will be yours, and I'll spend every day exorcising the pain of their loss."

To have a day without the sting of missing her family would be a dream. But some memories of the explosion couldn't be forgotten easily. They left permanent reminders. "My scars. How could you want—?"

"To look at your face?" Only two steps separated them now and Henry's eyes swam with quiet warmth. "Scars on the outside are not the dark ones. I don't see any part of you that isn't beautiful."

She laughed. "You're feeding me lines."

His face dropped as her blunt words hit. "Only the truth. I'll promise never to lie to you."

He closed the divide by a final step and with the tip of his finger, trailed her scar from start to finish, never breaking his gaze from hers until he realised he'd been too forward and he smiled apologetically.

Heavens be, he meant it. The softness of his calloused fingers surprised her, and she remembered how much she missed the touch of someone who cared for her. How her life was still filled with possibilities. After every trial she'd faced, perhaps a reprieve was due. She skirted the stairs and his touch. "May I have a moment?"

A gust of breeze kissed her cheeks, and a blush rose again. The cloth rustled in her hands, a reminder she neglected her work.

Henry ground the hat again before he flipped it back into shape. A bashful smile played his lips. "It's a big decision leaving what you know. I've had months to think about it. You've had minutes. Take the day. We're both late. I'll stop back tomorrow for your answer." He tipped his hat, the brim not quite as straight as usual, and strode to the road. The earth scuttled beneath his shoes when he turned back towards her. "I'll give you a good life. You'll want for nothing. Until tomorrow, Mabel."

He tipped his hat once more and disappeared out of sight while Mabel slumped dumbfounded onto the stairs, weighing the options presented to her.

~ ∂ ~

Spring came with a bustle of activity to keep Henry busy. Ice on the muddy riverbanks had thawed, blossoms coated the apple orchards and the new crop had been planted, so he passed the morning by shoring up the fence to keep the cows from escaping. Cerulean blue painted the sky, and the sun hammered its welcomed heat. He wiped at the sweat on his brow with the hem of his shirt, leant his arms on the fence and watched the river frolic with the field's edge. He'd spent miserable, damp nights in dreams of days such as this, and he couldn't help but sigh with contentment. Nothing compared.

After the task was finished, he meandered back to the house. At first glance, the front porch looked bare, but the scent of soap and whip of cloth in the breeze led him around the back. As he turned the corner, a faint hum caressed him: the tune of a song he often played on the piano in the front room. Sheets
46

billowed on the line and his shirts twisted, hiding her from sight. Only the faint etch of a shadow hinted at her location.

The grass swept beside his boots and stones rattled.

"The fence is fixed?" Mabel's voice floated to him.

"And the cattle are back," he replied as he saw her.

She smiled and clipped a pillowcase on the line.

"You've never sung before." Henry couldn't hide his surprise.

"I used to before..." She turned her head, so she could see him. "I don't know when I started again." She tucked the clothespins she held into the pocket of her apron and wiped her hands. "Take me on a walk along the river."

She held out her hand, which he swiftly clasped. The pale skin was a sharp contrast to a few months ago, soft and smooth like the petals of a mayflower. Time slowed on the path to the river. Bees brushed the apple blossoms, their buzz a faint, melodic background, and the floral scent flickered on the breeze.

"It's a lovely day," he said.

She flicked her gaze over the grass. "Is spring always like this in the valley?" Her nose crunched, and he wondered what grave her mind wandered to.

"Absolutely," he replied with a gentle nudge to her elbow. "Except when it rains."

His attempt at humour barely elicited a turn of her lips. They continued their walk.

She took a deep breath. "My grandparents went to service every morning, and that day mother went with them. Grandfather had hurt his leg the week before but refused to walk with a cane. Stubborn goat. There was nothing left of the church. My father was at the factory. He'd sent James on an errand and offered to take his place on the floor until he returned. The building collapsed, and everyone died. The same thing happened to my brothers, only they were in the school." She swallowed, stifling tears. "I kept picturing their death for the longest time. How the bell had rung and they placed their books on their desks, and then..." Her voice faded. "I lost everyone."

Henry squeezed her hand. He'd done the same thing when his

47

brothers died. Imagined their deaths in the bloodied earth, the pain of a bullet to the back, but he didn't tell her. Mabel hadn't spoken of her family before, and he absorbed every detail she shared.

"And you feel guilty for being the one who survived," he said.

She squeezed his hand back, and when she caught his eye, she smiled. "You were right you know. This place can exorcise the pain of ghosts. There's peace here."

They walked a few steps, then Henry dipped to pick a daisy. He snapped the stem to the right length, then tucked it amongst her wayward hair. "Yes, there is."

Mabel was a constant surprise, from how she'd waited on the step for him that autumn morning, bags packed, to the way she'd adapted so efficiently to farm life. He suspected she had many more to come, and he looked forward to every single one.

Polly J. Brown

Polly J. Brown writes stories of hope, and sometimes romance, with Atlantic Canadian connections. She lives on Nova Scotia's Eastern Shore with her husband, three children and an ever-changing number of pets. Her short story "Ever Be" was published in the *Story of a Kiss* Anthology.

When she isn't dreaming up new problems for her characters to solve, she can be found at the beach hunting for sea glass or searching for inspiration on the hiking trails.

The Whispers of Words

Diane Lynn McGyver

THE SOUND OF CLANKING METAL and grinding chains drifted through the open window and caught John's attention. He looked up from rinsing his cup and saw his son, Bill, had arrived to help clean out the garage. He released a sigh. If he were ten years younger, he'd tackle the job himself, but age caught up to him since his beloved Margaret had passed. One day they were laughing over tea and discussing the garden tomatoes and the next, he was placing a yellow rose on her coffin before they lowered it into the ground.

John watched Bill peer into the depths of the garage, not willing to go any farther less something tumbled out and snatch his life. He didn't blame him. He had been meaning to clean the garage for weeks, picking away at the things he could lift and toss into the garbage but each time he opened the door, the amount of stuff his family had gathered over the decades stifled him. Camping equipment, gardening tools, the kids' old bicycles, broken lawnmowers and snow blowers, miscellaneous tools and various items, lost, found and given, had found a home inside. His parents, who originally owned the property and lived out their years here, had contributed to the collection, but they had kept it tidy during their lifetime. If Pa could see the rubbish that had gathered since his death, he'd roll over in his grave.

The last time John could park his car inside was the winter before White Juan. He remembered it distinctly because his car—out in the elements—had been buried beneath an eight-foot drift. It had taken four days, three generous neighbours and Bill to set it free.

But today was the day. John placed the cup in the sink, slipped on his shoes and a sweater, and ambled out the back door.

"Dad," said Bill, turning around, "you've gotta be kidding me. It'll take a week of Sundays and all your kids to clear this mess."

John nodded. "It seems to have gotten out of hand."

"Out of hand? More like out of this world."

"No worries, Dad." Clare, Bill's wife, gave him a gentle hug. "This is not the first garage I've seen that wouldn't fit a car." She glanced at Bill with a knowing expression. "Mine has sat outside for three years."

Bill looked back at the garage. "Let's get started then."

For the next four hours, they dragged and carried sundry items out of the garage, making three piles in the driveway: keep, junk, sell. John helped where he could but at 81, he was not as youthful as he used to be. He took breaks often, offered tea or water and commented about surprise finds. "I haven't seen that since you were a boy, Bill," or "I remember the day I bought that. Your mother was crying because Elvis had passed." When Clare carried out a brown wooden box with a dial on it, he stood up and interrupted her trip to the junk pile.

"No, dear," he said. "I have to keep that."

"But it's old," she said. "Probably doesn't work."

"It was Pa's radio. It's a lucky charm." His father's voice spoke the words again inside his head. *It's a lucky charm.* John had heard it so often, at times he dreamt about it.

"One that has seen better days. I think we should throw it out."

"We can't."

"Is it valuable?"

"Extremely."

"A priceless antique?" Bill asked. "How much do you think it's worth?" He walked over and took a closer look.

"It's not for sale," John said. "Pa would never allow it."

Bill and Clare exchanged glances.

"I know what you're thinking," John said. "It's nothing of the sort. It's just..." He scratched his head as memories from long ago rushed in. The table-top transistor radio had rested in their kitchen his entire life until it stopped working shortly after Pa died in '98. It was as if they had both stopped working together.

"You're emotionally attached," Clare said.

"To junk?" Bill asked.

He shook his head. "Pa was superstitious."

"He was Irish," Bill said.

"What's that supposed to mean?" Clare adjusted the machine in her grip.

"You know." Bill shrugged. "Four-leaf clovers, pots of gold and horseshoes."

"Pa lived by this radio. He called it a wireless." John drew his hand gently across the top, leaving a mark in the dust. "He put his faith in it more than he did in God. It was on from the wee hours of the morning to deep into the night. He said he'd never live without the ability to know the current news." He looked up and grinned. "He was there, listening when the Hindenburg went down in 1937. He told us kids he had never heard anything more frightful on the radio than that live broadcast. The year before, when it had flown over Halifax, he was on the Citadel and had seen it."

"*The* Hindenburg?" Bill sounded sceptical.

John nodded. His father dreaded the drive to the city and complained each time he had to make the trip. He remembered him falling eerily silent as he left the house and the joy when he returned.

"I didn't know it flew over Nova Scotia," Clare said.

"July 4, 1936. It passed right overhead."

"Incredible." Bill looked at the radio closer. "Does it work?"

John shook his head. "Not for a while. I'd have to take it to an electrician."

Bill frowned. "It's past its prime, and you already have a good radio in the kitchen."

"I know." A wad of emotions stuck in his thoughts. His father loved this old radio and feared if it ever left the family, a tragic event might happen. John believed it stemmed from him being orphaned as a young lad and sent to Canada as a British Home Child. His father never talked about that time. John only knew he had no family, or none that came with him to Canada. "Pa needed to know the news as it happened," he said. "He was driven by a memory he wouldn't talk about."

Clare carried the radio to the small keep pile. "I'll set it here for now. If you change your mind, let me know."

John nodded, unable to take his eyes off the radio. His father would sit in the evenings and listen to the music and news reports. Early in the morning, he listened as he finished his tea. It was the last thing he did before he left for work. Once he retired, he continued to listen to the radio until 9:05 am, then he'd start his chores around the house. Why he waited until that odd time, John never knew.

One year, just before Christmas, when John was a young teen, he had entered the kitchen and found his father staring out the window with tears streaking his cheeks. John had held back and watched his mother embrace his father, speaking softly to him. He heard only a few words, but the ones that engraved themselves in his memory were, "They're watching from above, happy you survived." Who *they* were and what his father had survived, John never learned.

A few hours later, John was looking through a box of books, deciding if he wanted to read *West of the Pecos* by Zane Grey one more time or ship it to the Salvation Army Store. He recalled with great amusement many years ago when Pa told him the famous author of western novels had been named Pearl. It stuck in his head, and every time he heard Zane, he thought of a woman with her hair up in rollers.

"What is this?" Bill carried a strange container into the centre of the floor. "Looks like a trunk. An ancient one."

John placed the book in the keep pile and walked to his son to study the old straps that kept the lid tight on the odd box. It looked like a suitcase, but it was too tall. He had seen it before, he was certain, but it was so long ago, he could not remember the circumstances.

"What's inside?" Bill looked up expectantly.

John shrugged. "Your guess is as good as mine."

"You forgot?"

He shook his head. "I never knew."

"Isn't it your trunk?"

"I think it was Pa's."

"Really?" Bill took a closer look. "It's been here all these years and you've never looked inside?"

"I didn't know it was here."

"Put it on the table," Clare said. She pushed aside a box of old dishes to make room.

Bill set the trunk on the table and looked from one side of it to the other. "How do you open it?"

John ran his hand along the front, noticed the release clips and pressed them. To his surprise, they snapped up, releasing the lid. Inside, surrounded by old clothes was a shoebox. The design appeared to be decades old. Scribbled across the top in marker on dried masking tape was the name *William McDonald*.

"Could it be yours, Bill?" Clara asked.

"Not mine," he said. "Probably Granddad's." He looked at his father for confirmation.

"Has to be." John pulled the lid off the shoebox and saw a hardcover book inside. He opened the cover and on the first page he read, *The Great Adventures of William McDonald*.

"Granddad was a writer?" asked Bill.

"I never saw him write." John turned the page and saw dates and paragraphs. "It's a journal."

"A diary?" Clara asked.

"It appears to be." John adjusted his glasses and read the first entry. "*Tuesday June 19th, 1917. Father took me to the waterfront to see the ships. More than a month has passed since I last visited the harbour and I was stunned at the number of new vessels that had arrived. The biggest surprise was seeing the ship filled with soldiers going overseas to fight in the war. Father said he was glad I was too young to go, but this confused me. The soldiers and sailors boasted about going and were always smiling when they walked up the gangplank. When I told mother I wanted to join the army and go to England, she told me to stay in school. That's where I belonged as I was only nine."*

John huffed. "This can't be Pa's book. He never knew his parents."

"So another William McDonald." Bill frowned. "There are thousands of us around. Dad, did you and Mom think of that when you gave me the name?"

He grinned. "I named you after my father. It was tradition." His smiled faded. "Do you think it was any easier being John McDonald?"

"Fair enough." Bill pointed to the shoebox. "So why do you have *this* William McDonald's stuff? Could he be a relative? An uncle?"

"Pa didn't have a brother or a sister." He thought for a moment. "Perhaps it was given to Pa by mistake."

Clare gently turned a few pages. "Whoever this William was, he wrote every day. Here he talks about his little sister, Sarah. She said her first words on July 7th. He had a brother named John. He was eight." She looked closer, read for a moment, then announced, "He lived on Windmill Road in Dartmouth."

"Dartmouth?" Bill's face bent in confusion. "What's this box doing in Pictou?"

John shrugged as he bent to look at the writing. A pain in his leg reminded him of his arthritis and he straightened. "What else does it say?"

Clare flipped a few more pages. "He said his sister Sarah called him Booboo." She looked at Bill and smiled. "Don't you have an Aunt Sarah?"

He nodded. "Dad's older sister."

"Strange." She read more. "He started school on September 6th. He was in grade three. Here it says he turned ten on September 24th."

"Isn't that Granddad's birthday?" Bill asked.

John nodded. The information swirled in his head, making

him dizzy. Who was this William McDonald? He reached for a chair and almost stumbled.

"Here, Dad." Bill steadied him and helped him to sit. "Maybe we should put this away to look at later."

"There's a family picture," Clare said, her voice rising. She pulled out an old black and white image measuring roughly 5x7 inches. "The names are on the back. William and Kathleen McDonald. The children were William, John, Sarah and Aileen."

John swallowed hard. "I have sisters named Aileen and Kathleen." The dust in the garage swirled in the light breeze, and he stared at the dust devils in hope to make sense of the similar names. Clare held the photo out to him and he studied the faces. They were family. He recognised the hair, the noses, the eyes and chins. But how? Who were they?

"Did your father ever mention the Halifax Explosion?" Clare had returned to the book. "On the morning of December 6th, William didn't go to school. John and Kathleen were home sick and he didn't want to go alone, so he went to his favourite spot on the lake. He was sitting there writing in this book when the terrible explosion happened."

John looked up, dazed. "But..." His mouth hung open and scattered memories gathered like pieces of a puzzle. His father had never lived in Dartmouth, yet he knew things about the harbour. Occasionally, he'd mention so-and-so living near Halifax Harbour and wonder why they'd live so close to it.

"The December 6th entry ends in mid-sentence with a long pencil mark, as if he was startled." She held up the book to show him, then turned it around to read. "December 7th, 1917, he writes, *It's the most horrible sight. They are gone. The house is in pieces. Mother and the wee one born only days ago, and John and Sarah and Aileen. They are all gone. Father has not been home since the ship blew up. I cannot cry more. I am alone and Mr. Dixon says Father might not return. He was on the waterfront working on a boat. I will wait for them. They must come home. It is a bad dream. I can't go on alone.*" She wiped away a tear and sniffed. "I can't imagine what the boy felt. I can feel his heart break though it happened almost a hundred years ago."

Bill put his arm around her shoulders. "Maybe his father survived."

Clare dabbed her eyes and continued to read. "December 8th, 2017. *Mrs. Dixon told me she wanted to throw out my clothes because she could not remove the smell of smoke, but I stopped her. Mother had made them for me. It was all I had left of her. The Dixons are a nice family. They have eight kids. Mrs. Dixon's mother also lives in the house. I am sleeping on the floor in the parlour until Father returns. We will have to find somewhere else to live. Old Mr. Carter was found alive this morning.*" She looked up hopeful. "Maybe he did survive."

Bill pulled a piece of clothing from the trunk and held it up. It was a woollen pair of pants. "A perfect fit for a skinny ten-year-old boy."

"It's incredible they survived." She turned the page. "December 9th, 2017. *It is with great sadness I must write these words for my heart can barely stand the ache. A policeman came and told Mr. Dixon they had found Father's body. My family is gone.*"

John hung his head. His father had been an orphan after all. The worst kind. One who remembered and loved his family dearly.

"He's sent to River John," Clare said.

"That's where Pa grew up."

"He wrote, *Mr. Dixon's friend has a farm in River John. He needs help and offered me a home. I don't want to leave my family, but there is no room in the Dixon home for me. It is for the best. I cannot sleep and I have bad dreams. Sometimes I can see Mother tucking me in. She smiles at me and tells me everything will be all right.*"

A newspaper article slipped from between the pages. Bill picked it up. "It's from the *Halifax Herald*. The headline reads, *Halifax Wrecked. More than one thousand killed in this city, many thousands are injured and homeless.* It says the *Mont-Blanc* exploded at 9:05."

John stared at the radio sitting in the driveway. The sun shone upon it creating a halo-like glow. He wondered if his father thought of that day long ago every time he switched it on. If families had had radios on December 6, 1917, they would have been warned to stay away from the shoreline. They could have run to safety. Hundreds could have been saved. William Sr. could have raced home, and he and Kathleen could have gathered the children and went to the lake where William Jr. sat writing. He tried to clear his throat, but the lump brought tears to his eyes. The father he loved and admired had kept this secret for himself to endure. If only John had suspected, he could have tried to ease his pain. He could do nothing now except learn about the family he never knew.

Three months later on September 24th...

John held the container of dirt in his shaky hands. He glanced around at the faces of his siblings, children, grandchildren, nieces and nephews who gathered around the simple headstone engraved with the names of his grandparents, aunts and uncles. Clare had found the graves through researching at the pubic archives. The McDonald family—William Sr., Kathleen, John, Sarah, Aileen and baby Patrick—had been laid to rest at Tufts Cove Cemetery, not far from where William Jr. had been writing in his journal that fatal day. The boy would have been 110 years old today. Earlier, they had visited his grave, spoke a few words and gathered the container of dirt. They spread it here, then scooped up a sample to take to William Jr.'s grave. It was a mixing of dirt, a connection to bring the family together long after they had been separated.

"He was the strongest man I knew," John said in a hoarse voice. He glanced at his sisters, Kathleen, Sarah and Aileen, and his brother Patrick. "We can't undo the past. We can only honour it and hope for a better future."

Diane Lynn McGyver

Diane Lynn McGyver grew up along the wild shores of Nova Scotia. She spent her summers running barefoot through the forest and sailing on the sea, and her winters building snow forts, skating and playing hockey. She began writing at an early age, filling Campfire Notebooks with tales based on her imagination and her adventures.

She dwells on a small homestead where she raises children, Toggenburg goats and chickens. Her work has appeared in more than a thousand publications since 1997.

She is the author of *Shadows in the Stone*, *Scattered Stones*, *Twistmas*, *Fowl Summer Nights* and *Nova Scotia – Life Near Water*. To learn more about her books, visit her website at https://dianelynnmcgyver.com.

The Ring

Cheryl Lynn Davis

SHE SHOULD STAND UP, GO to the sink, pretend she was about to conquer the mound of dishes accumulating since yesterday; pretend she had a plan for the rest of the day that stretched before her; pretend the sound of Angela's key in the lock was interrupting...*what? Something. Anything.* But even a pretense took effort, and Ellie hadn't felt the desire to put effort into anything for six months.

Since Mark died.

Like the epitaph on her late husband's headstone, the words were carved into her mind. She imagined herself a cartoon character with one of those comic speech balloons hanging over her head, only her one-liner wasn't a witticism but a verdict, *a life sentence.*

Since Mark died. The passage of time no longer began with her birth but with his death.

"Hey. How was your day?" Angela dropped her purse and jacket on the kitchen table, her eyes taking in the mess Ellie *hadn't* cleaned.

For the first three months, her sister wouldn't have dreamt of asking Ellie how her day was, knowing the answer, but it seemed Angela no longer believed compassion and sympathy were helping as her tone nearly always bordered on irritation these days.

"I see you kept yourself busy."

And there it was. Angela's incrimination, though both expected and deserved, brought tears to Ellie's eyes. "I'm sorry."

Angela looked at her and sighed. "I know." She sank into the chair opposite her. "I know it's hard, Ell, I do, but you moved back to Halifax for a fresh start. It's not going to just happen. *You have to make it happen!*" She reached across the table and clasped Ellie's hands in hers. "It's been six months and you haven't even looked for a job yet. The insurance from Mark's car accident will only last so long."

Ellie looked away. The words echoed in her head, and she wondered if it was because she'd heard them so many times.

"I know he was the love of your life, but you *will* find somebody else."

Ellie mutely shook her head.

"Yes, you will," Angela said firmly. "But not inside my apartment. I love having you here, but I can't watch you wither away. You have to keep living."

"I am living," she protested feebly.

"No, you're not," Angela said softly.

"I'm just tired." She rubbed her eyes, an unconscious reaction to the words. "I had another dream last night."

"Another dream?"

"The same dream."

Ellie wasn't going to mention the dream, but she needed to distract her sister. The paranormal was Angela's *thing*; ghosts, dreams, tarot cards and spirits were an obsession with her. She kept a Ouija Board from their childhood tucked away in her closet. When they were kids, she would drag Ellie to the Halifax Ghost Walk *every year*, and they'd already visited most of Nova Scotia's *alleged* haunted houses.

Ellie nodded, relieved the diversion was working. "It was different though, more intense. She's becoming stronger. Last night, she reached for me. It looked like she was covered in blood." *She* being the girl in her dreams.

"And?"

"There was blood dripping from her fingers, but the rest of

her was covered in black oil, soot or something."

"Do you see what you're doing to yourself?" Angela jokingly chided. "You're starting to sound like me."

The comment elicited a small smile from Ellie. "At least I'm not frightened of her anymore. She's becoming familiar in a strange sort of way."

"What do you mean?"

"I'm not sure, but I wish I knew what she wanted. It's hard enough to get a sound sleep without having to deal with that." Before Mark passed away, she slept the sleep of the dead. Any dreams that managed to penetrate her catatonic slumber were forgotten before she swiped the snooze button on her cellphone. But this one was vivid and recurring, which disturbed her more than she let on. She'd offered this up as a diversion but in truth, she was hoping her sister could make some sense out of it for her. "How does it happen, Ange?"

"How does what happen?"

"How does your subconscious mind create a person in your dreams? Where does it draw the details? Things you know, what you feel, all of these things get stored in your memory and processed by the brain; how then does a complete stranger manifest itself into your subconscious?"

"I don't know. We're spiritual beings. Maybe she's trying to talk to you."

Ellie knew her diversion was complete when her sister next spoke.

"Let's have a séance?" Angela's eyes were shining, clearly excited by the prospect.

"No." Ellie forced herself to her feet and headed for the coffee pot buried behind last night's supper plates.

"It might help; maybe we can rid you of your ghost."

"She's not a ghost. It's a dream."

"Do you remember when we were kids, how much fun we had having a séance?"

"You had fun. I was always scared to death; half way through the night, I'd be crawling into your bed."

"Recurring dreams usually mean something."

"It means I'm drinking too much coffee." Ellie drained the pot into a large red mug, then stirred in sugar and milk.

"Seriously, Ellie, you might be able to talk to her through a séance."

Or maybe I could talk to Mark? Like a vein of gold through a mountain of rock, the thought wound through her deadened emotions, laying spark to the part of her that had died with her husband. She held her tongue, knowing it wasn't a hope Angela would encourage and nodded her agreement.

Angela placed four white candles fortuitously on the coffee table. She set the wicks to flame and turned off the two side lamps, adding clarity to their cosy apartment. The resulting yellow glow inhaled the room, leaving pockets of shadows in its wake. The sweet smell of sandalwood hung heavily in the air, infiltrating Ellie's senses to a point that was almost offensive. She thought about objecting to the incense burners but knew it would be futile. The Ouija Board sat on the coffee table, the heart-shaped planchette on top, waiting for quivering fingertips.

Her sister knelt beside the table and patted the empty floor in front of her, beckoning Ellie over. Ellie giggled nervously but did as requested. Sinking onto the plush carpet, she folded her legs beneath her as Angela had done and rested her hands on her thighs. Her sister's gravity unnerved her. *Did Angela really think this was going to work?* Ellie had acquiesced to the séance in a desperate attempt to reach Mark but found herself enjoying the return to their childhood. As frightened as she had been back then, she'd enjoyed playing out the charade with Angela. *And what if it did work?* She found herself grasping at the possibility.

"Close your eyes, picture the girl from the dream, try to draw her to us." Angela directed.

Ellie did as bidden, conjuring Mark's image from precious memories. It distressed her to realise at some point, she would forget what he looked like.

She felt the solidity of the Ouija board as her sister balanced it across the breadth of their legs. In a firm but soothing voice,

Angela began the séance.

"Let our spirit guides protect us from negative energies as we call forth the woman from my sister's dreams."

Ellie focussed intently on repressing the woman and held tight to Mark's image. Dark hair, brown eyes, his soft caress on her upper arm; the pain of remembering was piercing.

"You can open your eyes now," Angela said. She manoeuvred the planchette in a circular motion around the board before allowing it to rest. "Put your fingers on the planchette lightly; don't press on it."

Ellie followed her sister's lead and placed her fingers on the plastic piece.

"Are you ready?"

She gulped and nodded.

"Spirit, are you here with us now?"

Angela didn't sound frightened, not like Ellie whose stomach was flip-flopping. Her breath caught in her throat when the planchette crept across the board. "Are you doing that?" A tinge of anger laced her words, but her sister didn't answer.

Angela's eyes were as wide as toonies, and Ellie could see some of her own panic reflected in them. When the planchette hovered over *YES*, she stared at Ellie.

"Did you move it?" she whispered.

Ellie shook her head.

Angela swallowed and turned her attention back to the board. "What is your name, spirit?"

The planchette moved again, this time faster. Ellie followed its course: D-O-R-A a slight pause, then H-A-M-L-I-N.

"Dora Hamlin!"

"I don't know anybody named Dora," Ellie whispered.

"You don't have to know her," Angela whispered back.

"Ask her why she keeps bothering me?"

The candles flickered beneath the weight of one solid breeze, a hair's breadth from extinguishment before flaring back to life.

"Dora, are you the girl in Ellie's dreams?"

Their fingers trembled over the heart-shaped planchette as it

63

once again settled on the word *YES*.

"Do you want something from her?" Angela continued.

Ellie tensed, afraid of the answer. The planchette crept around the board, the clear plastic circle in the middle highlighting individual letters.

"*My what?*" Ellie bent closer to the board to see better. "Did she say *my ring*?"

The planchette flew to the word *YES*, their fingers nearly losing touch with it, it travelled so fast.

"I don't know what ring she's talking about." Ellie was defensive. "The only ring I wear is my wedding ring, and she's not getting it."

The planchette went crazy, swirling around faster and faster until it flew off the board and landed with a soft thud on the carpet. Afraid of the dark energy, Ellie and Angela bolted, crawling in haste to the far side of the room. The Ouija board was left discarded behind them. Breathing loudly, they stared at each other. Then Angela laughed.

"We did it! We talked to the dead!"

Ellie stood up on shaky legs. "I don't think it's so funny. You did that, didn't you? You moved that thing all around the board."

Angela's grin fell away. "I didn't." She stood beside Ellie. "I swear I didn't. I know these dreams are freaking you out. I wouldn't do that, seriously."

Ellie walked to the couch and sat down. The tears that filled her eyes annoyed her. "What is going on? I don't understand this."

Angela shook her head. "I'm not sure. I've used this Ouija Board many times, and I've never had this happen." She sunk into the couch beside her. "You have her ring."

"Oh, Jesus." Ellie pressed her fingertips to her eyebrows. "I'm exhausted."

They sat for a few moments in silence, each pondering the incredulity of what had happened. Angela finally stood and blew out the candles. She stubbed the end of the incense into the holder before laying it flat in the cradle. Grabbing the blanket off the moon chair, she offered it to Ellie.

"Just lay back; try to get some rest here on the couch. Maybe she only comes to people who sleep in beds." Angela offered a feint grin.

Needing little persuasion, Ellie lay back, pulling the blanket to her chin. Her eyelids fluttered as she watched Angela gather the Ouija Board and take it to her bedroom. When she reappeared to shut the lights off, Ellie's eyes flew open, expecting to see Dora standing before her.

"It's just me," Angela whispered. "Go back to sleep."

Ellie complied. Tonight, she thought, tonight there will be no dreams.

It was early for Dora Hamlin to be out and about. The night's sky had only just given way to the new day, and she found she hadn't dressed well enough for the seasonal cold embracing her fingers through woollen mitts. She knew it was past 7:30 because the ships anchored at the mouth of the harbour were beginning their slow progression towards the Bedford Basin.

Turning from Russell Street onto Campbell Road, she was both anxious and relieved at the same time; her destination, the distant grey mass of the Acadia Sugar Refinery, gave the illusion of being close, but Dora knew she would have to hasten her steps if she wanted to catch Thomas before his 8:00 am shift.

She ran until her breath felt squeezed from her chest, slowing to a walk long enough to get it back and then ran again. Mother would know she was gone now. After their quarrel last night, she also would have guessed Dora had run straight to Thomas this morning. Her mother's refusal to allow her and Thomas to marry made no sense. She was 21; most girls were getting married at this age, if not married already.

You'll have more suitors, Dora, men that are more of your station, she had said.

Dora knew that wasn't true. She wasn't like the other girls, not as smart, nor as pretty. People had always gazed at her as though they were trying to figure something out, and she always knew when they did. Their look of bewilderment transformed into a gentle smile, encouraged by their secret knowledge of her lack of intellect. Only Thomas thought she was brilliant, her Thomas.

Anger and frustration creased the smooth skin of her forehead and forced her normally upturned lips into a scowl. Her steps became more defiant, more purposeful as she half ran, half walked down Campbell Road towards the refinery.

The streets of Halifax were busy at this early hour; soldiers with duffle bags slung over their shoulders and merchants intent on their destination brushed past her with nary a backward glance. Most of her neighbours worked here in the Richmond district, and Dora kept her eyes downcast, not wanting to meet up with any of them. After what seemed an indeterminable amount of time, the refinery's eight-storey building rose up in front of her, and she breathed a sigh of relief.

Employees passed her as she stood waiting on the side of the street. She recognised a few of them and shyly murmured a greeting; if she were to be Thomas's wife, she would need to know these people and be nice to them.

"Are you looking for Thomas?"

The voice startled Dora and she jumped. The man had come up from the pier and was holding a crate filled with burlap sacks. Locked into her own thoughts, she hadn't seen him approach.

"Yes." She flushed, feeling she should have said more than the one word.

"He's inside. I'll get him for you."

"Thank you." Her mother would have used her lack of social grace to support the argument she was not yet ready to marry. How could she be a proper wife when she was barely able to talk to men? A proper wife—a nervous fear crept up her back—she knew what that meant. It was more than the kisses Thomas gave her that left her tingling and unsure of herself.

"Dorey?" Thomas hurried towards her. "Why are you here? Is there something wrong?"

"Oh, Thomas!" She threw herself at him and cried. "Mother says I can't marry you; she says you don't have enough money. She says I'm not old enough and smart enough to be a wife yet."

"There, there, Dorey." He softly spoke his pet name for her. He

stroked her back until she calmed a bit. "I'll talk to your mother; I'll make her understand."

"But she won't, Thomas. I know she won't. She says I need to be looked after." The sobbing started again.

He lifted her quivering chin with one hand and dug into his pocket with the other. "I have something for you. I was going to wait until after work to give it to you, but since you're here..."

She blinked rapidly to push the tears from her eyes, so she could see. He held a ring in his hand, a slim band of gold with a pearl stone.

"It's an engagement ring, Dorey. You show your mother this. You tell her if I can buy you this, then I can take care of you."

Her eyes widened. A ring just like other girls wore. He grasped her right hand and prepared to slip the ring onto her finger.

"No, Thomas, it goes on the left hand."

"Oh." He pursed his lips together and rolled his eyes, eliciting a giggle from her. He switched hands. "Dora Hamlin, will you be my wife? Will you be Mrs. Thomas Davies?"

She flushed. "Yes, Thomas, of course I will."

"They're going to collide!" A man shouted from the pier, interrupting their moment.

They turned to where he pointed. On the Dartmouth side of the harbour, two ships were signaling to each other for passage. Dora glanced at Thomas; his gentle face had gathered worry lines and the sparkle in his eyes dimmed.

"It's not right," he said, and she followed his gaze back to the ships.

Both vessels continued to whistle, but neither seemed to pay heed to the other. A crowd had gathered on the docks to view the spectacle, and she imagined they would all be talking about it at the dinner table that night.

A cracking noise reverberated across the harbour, echoing into the air where it hung for a few seconds before fading. A collective gasp ran as if a wave through the gaping crowd as all realised the two ships had collided. Dora heard somebody say it was a munitions ship, and then the popping sound began. The onlookers *were pleased, applauding the display. Dora herself laughed and clapped her hands with delight.*

"Go!" It was Thomas, shoving her to the street. "You have to leave."

"But I want to watch," she protested.

"No, Dora, go!" He kept looking back over his shoulder. The pops were coming closer together now. He could see the crewmembers of one ship scrambling over the side into a lifeboat. Dora pushed back against him; she didn't want to miss what everybody else would see.

Thomas grabbed her by the shoulders, his fingers digging into her soft skin. "Dora, you're mother needs to know I can take care of you, right?"

She frowned but nodded.

"Well, she would be awfully angry if she knew you were here, and I didn't send you home, wouldn't she?"

She glanced again at the two ships in the harbour, the fire in the hold of one growing at an alarming rate. He was right, it would do her no good to stay and have her mother find out.

"Okay," she lamented.

"Go," he said. "I want you to run, Dora, run as fast as you can."

The tone of his voice frightened her. She stumbled backwards onto the street and ran.

~ ✂ ~

Ellie woke, her heart thudding loudly in her chest, her breath ragged, her senses acute. Unable to relax in the same room where they'd had the séance, she had staggered to her bedroom where she'd fallen asleep only to slip into Dora's world again. Glancing wildly around her room for the source of the loud explosion, the unexpected composure of her bedroom baffled her. The blinds were drawn with only the slightest of colour variance outlining their square shape. It wasn't morning yet or the muted grey seeping around the edges of the blind would be white or a shade thereof. As it was, the room was cloaked in darkness.

Her heart beat thunderous in her ears as she fought to still its erratic rhythm. *Blood, she could see blood.* Stains of red were everywhere. It ran down the white dresser tucked into the corner. The curtains shimmered with its ruby colour, and the bed linens were damp and odourous from its sticky texture. She shook her head to dislodge the vision. The room was dark. She couldn't really see anything, *could she*?

Indistinguishable shapes materialized in the shadows of the night. Her bureau, white in the light of day, was a grey mass, with the lamp she'd purchased from Bouclair steadfast on its topside. *It was a dream*, she told herself, *just another dream*. But this one was different; it was no longer of Dora herself. In slow motion, a fragment from Dora's life had unravelled inside Ellie's subconscious. The frenetic pace of the young girl's anxiety had stolen her sense of self, and she'd found herself floating on the edges of Dora's life.

Reality grasped at her with ice-cold tentacles. Ellie struggled to a sitting position, her breath labored. She needn't fight to hold onto the details of the dream; they were as vivid as though she'd been walking the street herself. Instinct told her it was Halifax. There'd been no bridges, and the three red and white-striped towers from Tufts Cove Generating Station had been notably absent, but it was one of those vague certainties one knows when they are in the midst of a dream.

The vision had been a myriad of emotions: sadness, anxiety, happiness and then *fear*. Ellie pulled her knees up and hugged them to her chest. *Poor Dora*. What had happened to her? Thomas's proposal told Ellie he felt the same way as Dora. Why had Dora felt such paralyzing fear?

And then with acute clarity, Ellie snapped fully awake. *The ring*. She scrambled from the bed, grabbed the little wooden box sitting on the top of the dresser and flung the lid open. *There it was*.

The gold band embedded with a small but exquisite pearl peeked up at her. Buried by plastic cosmetic jewelry, she'd forgotten about it until now. Tenderly she picked it up and her eyes welled with tears. The band was warm, simmering energy beneath her touch. It had been dull, lacklustre when she'd stumbled across it at the flea market six weeks ago. She knew a little warm water and dish soap would ease the passage of time, and she'd been pleased the seller accepted eight dollars for it.

She hurried down the short hall to Angela's room and threw open the door. Dropping to her knees beside her sister's bed, she shook her awake.

"What, what's wrong?" Angela's eyes struggled to open.

"I found it," Ellie said. "I found the ring."

There was no sleeping after that. Angela thought a mug of warm milk would help so they gathered in the kitchen, Ellie's laptop open in front of her.

"So what do we do with it? How do we give a ring back to a dead person?"

Ellie clicked on the Internet icon and waited for it to load. "We know she's dead, right?"

"Yes." Angela slid her chair closer.

"Historical Vital Statistics. If I'm right and it is Halifax I saw in my dream, there is a death certificate online for her."

Angela's face expanded with excitement. She pressed into Ellie's right shoulder as anxious fingers took flight over the keyboard. *Dora Hamlin.* Click Enter. And wait.

"There's a lot there." Ellie chewed her bottom lip, her eyes scanning the names. "No," she shook her head, "the dates don't fit."

"You're on marriages; check the deaths."

Another click as they waited, breathless with anticipation.

"Damn." Ellie's rigid shoulders fell and she sank back into the chair. "Of course it couldn't be that easy. There's a D Hamlin but nothing in 1917, and I'm sure it happened during the Halifax Explosion."

"Don't be too discouraged. We'll come up with another way to find it."

With a morose face, Ellie stared at the laptop a little longer. "I thought we had it." She stood up. "We'll go the archives. Hopefully they'll have something."

"Yes, and the library. The more we know about the Explosion, the better." Angela squeezed her sister's shoulder in sympathy.

"We're not giving up. We'll look again when I get home from work. Now, let's get some sleep. I have to work in a few hours."

Back in her room, Ellie eased herself into the warmth of her muddled blankets. Angela was right. It was too early to get discouraged. Now that she had a name, Dora was much less frightening.

～ ֎ ～

Dora heard voices, tumescent sounds like those heard when you're submersed in water. A child was crying, and somewhere to her right a woman called for Samuel. Who was Samuel, she wondered; her son, her husband, maybe a brother? There were other voices, wails of despair that twisted around one another until braiding themselves into a united chorus of anguish and sorrow.

Dora lay still, listening to them, too afraid to move as Samuel's name became George, George became Catherine and Catherine became Ann. She waited patiently for it to become Dora, knowing it would be her mother's voice she'd hear. It would be rife with worry at first, fading quickly to anger due to Dora's disobedience and her frantic flight to see Thomas. Thomas. Her heart pulsed.

She would rather it be Thomas's voice. If he found her, it would be romantic. Better yet, her mother would be so appreciative for saving her daughter's life, she wouldn't dare stop them from marrying. Yes, Thomas's voice would be better. She had only to lie still a while longer and he would be here.

So she waited, through Dickie and Ruth and Bert and Richard and Lillian and Hilary. She heard plaintive cries for James and Bessie and Hattie and Mary and even a Ziggy, but no one called for Dora. How much longer would she have to wait? What if Thomas never came? What if her mother, so angry with her for sneaking out before daybreak, had abandoned her!

Or maybe, and the thought, persistent since she'd regained consciousness, morphed into a terrifying possibility; maybe they were hurt and needed her assistance.

The thought was enough to break the disabling fear that had cocooned her. With trepidation, she opened her eyes. Mud clung to her lashes, heavy on her lids, and she blinked several times.

71

Everything was so dark. How long had she lain here waiting?

She pulled her knees up and reached out with her arms to leverage herself. A splintering pain shot up through to her left shoulder. Rolling onto her buttocks, she looked down at her dangling limb. From elbow to wrist, it was crushed, and her hand had somehow contorted to face the wrong direction. Lying still, it had gone unnoticed but now, having finally found the courage to move, it was like a knife splicing her arm in two. She would need help if she were to find Thomas and her family.

Tear-filled eyes cast their gaze, searching for rescue, but what she saw drained her of hope. A petrified landscape besieged her. The acrid smell of burning wood seared her nostrils, and fires raged everywhere. The houses! Where were all the houses! Timber upon timber heaped upon itself, like discarded lumber at the mill. Struggling to her feet, blazing heat from the fires scorched the air around her.

Had the Germans done this? The possibility made her sick, and she vomited until her stomach emptied and she was left with only dry heaves to contend with. Mustering her courage and realising no good would come of her standing there, she picked her way over the thickly strewn rubble of what was once a thriving Richmond. At Thomas' urging, she had fled, running down Campbell Road as if a rabid dog had been chasing her. What had frightened him?

She remembered then, the two ships in the harbour, the collision and the masses of bystanders whose insipid lives had been bolstered by the excitement of something different. Where had they all gone? Which way was the sugar refinery?

There was no clear path through the wreckage of houses. Campbell Road was gone, the whole area flattened. Dora winced as something sharp pierced through the sole of her boot. She bent to remove it, noted the soot covering her footwear, and was shocked to realise she had no boots on. Her bare feet were sheathed in what appeared to be black oil. Frantically she swiped at it, but the area to be cleaned grew more expansive. Even more shocking, she discovered her entire body was devoid of clothing and covered in the same blackness. Crying, she searched for something to cover herself with. From beneath a mound of splintered wood, a triangle of woollen material peeked out. She grabbed it with her right hand and jerked, but the item remained steadfast. She jerked again. This time the coat loosened, sending her backwards onto more wreckage. Agony racked her body as she landed on her broken arm.

Dora crawled to the cloth and was pleased to find it was a man's coat, long enough to cover her naked bottom. She jostled it about until it was positioned enough for her right arm to slide in, but there was something obstructing the sleeve hole. Shaking the coat, she tried to dislodge the obstruction, but it held firm. Using her feet to anchor the garment, she reached in, grasped the impediment and pulled. It was an arm, severed from shoulder to elbow. She held the appendage, too horrified to do anything but stare at it. A loud keening sound filled her ears, and she realised it was her voice she heard. Her wailing broke her paralysis, and she dropped the amputated limb onto a nearby pile of planks.

The pain in her arm was forgotten in her panic to get away. Scrambling over the wreckage of Richmond, she left the coat and the arm behind her. Shadows, hidden in the gloom, moaned as she passed them. Huddled masses took shape in the carnage and names once more resounded in the silence. She was heading for the harbour, but the smell of the sea evaded her and only her downhill descent told her she was heading in the right direction. As she staggered through the grey landscape, she stumbled over mangled and bloody bodies. Those that were alive were like apparitions, experiencing their own horrific purgatory, every one of them bleeding or missing limbs, most of them as naked as she was.

When the ground levelled, she stopped to take heed of her surroundings. She looked down at the water swirling about her ankles. The harbour. She was here; what else could explain the water? But where were the buildings. Looking in all directions, an unobstructed view with only a dark grey sky presented itself.

Dear God, she thought, everything is gone.

~ ✣ ~

It wasn't necessary to go to the Halifax Archives; the Internet was full of information on the Halifax Explosion, and Ellie found a published list of the dead on the archive's website. As she scrolled through *The Halifax Explosion Remembrance Book*, the horror of that day became incomprehensible to her: babies, whole families, gone. Her throat constricted when she found Thomas' name; the online book listed Thomas Davies as an employee of the Acadia Sugar Refinery, *body unfound*.

Dora's Thomas.

Ellie fought the lump in her throat. With no body, it would be like forever waiting for him to walk back into her life, just appear one day as if he'd gone for milk. At least with Mark, she had closure.

How to begin when you've no end? For that's what she imagined it was like for Dora, years upon years of waiting to wake up from this horrible nightmare. Sixteen years to be exact. She'd found Dora's death certificate on the vital statistics site shortly after waking. The Hamlin family had survived the Explosion; both parents outlived Dora who died of tuberculous in 1933. She was buried in Fairview Cemetery.

The urgency to get Dora's ring back to her couldn't be ignored. Yanking on a coat, she left the apartment, caught the bus from Clayton Park to Connaught Street and walked the short distance to the graveyard. The air was crisp, cool for this early in the fall. Ellie trudged the length of the sidewalk, her coat pulled tightly about her. The ring was tucked away in her pocket, wrapped in a small, square piece of felt her sister used for cleaning her computer screen. Ellie kept her hand pressed against it, fearful it would disappear, but it's presence in her pocket was palpable.

She'd called ahead for the plot number, scribbling down the directions, but they were embedded into her memory. It pleased her to find the stone in fairly good condition; so many of the older stones she'd passed were in various states of decay, their inscriptions illegible.

Dora Hamlin, beloved daughter. 1896-1933. Her breath was tight in her chest as she knelt upon the patch of grass in front the stone. Sitting back on her heels, she wondered how she was going to do this. She could bury it, but she hadn't thought of bringing tools with her, and if anybody saw her digging at a grave, it wouldn't go over well.

"I'm sorry for what happened to you," Ellie whispered. "I wish you and Thomas had more time together." She reached out, running her fingers along the inscription. "But I have what you want. I hope it gives you peace." She retrieved the ring, removed it from its covering and stuffed the felt back into her pocket. Standing up, she placed it on the top of the headstone and stepped back. "Thomas loved you, Dora."

Ellie turned and walked a few hundred metres before realising her stupidity. Somebody would take the ring, or a strong wind could blow it away. The only way she would know it was safe was to bury it. She cursed herself for not thinking to bring tools with her. But a sharp rock could unearth enough dirt to cover it, and the act would be less conspicuous. There was a slim one with a bit of a point, enough to break the earth, a few steps away. She bent, grabbed it and hurried back to Dora.

The top of the headstone was smooth, empty; *the ring was gone*. Ellie was frantic, threading her fingers through the grass, digging into the crevice at the base of the marker, but she found nothing. The ring was gone. It was impossible; only seconds had passed since she'd placed the gold band on the headstone.

Realisation dawned on her; Dora had taken it. The first genuine smile since Mark had died flitted across her face. She felt unburdened, empowered by the knowledge Dora now had closure. With so little time spent with Thomas, Dora's memories were few but the ring was symbolic, evidence of their love.

For the first time since Mark's car accident, she felt herself letting go of her own grief, feeling blessed for the many memories she and her husband had made during their eight years together. It wasn't the lifetime they'd planned but it was a life, and it was a happy life.

Dora had her ending. And now Ellie had a beginning.

Cheryl Lynn Davis

First published in a variety of magazines, Cheryl Lynn Davis has changed her focus to the fictional narrative. *The Ring* is her second sojourn into the world of historical fiction, the first being a short story set in Kansas in the late 1880s. She is currently working on her first full-length manuscript, *The Broken Child*.

Bluebirds and Daisies

Bronwen Piper

LORENA BRODY ADJUSTED HER WHITE veil, then fastened the top button on her overcoat. The brisk breeze blowing off the water stole beneath her long coat and skirt and brought a chill to her core. It brushed against her cheeks and cooled them in spite of her earlier thoughts of the handsome sailor who had caused them to warm. The crossing from Dartmouth to Halifax was almost complete, and soon she'd be in a warm building, listening to lectures on how to attend the sick and injured and then putting those lessons into practice in the afternoon as she worked alongside an experienced nurse.

After almost ten months of nursing instruction, she was unsure if this was the profession she desired to dedicate her life to. She cared about people, but the deeply personal care she was expected to deliver stirred unpleasant feelings in her stomach and at times produced uncomfortable dreams. The ghastliest being last night when she had entered a ward and found a body covered with a white sheet. She had instinctively lifted the sheet and stiffened. Lying on the cold, dirt-covered table was her older brother, Wallis, still in uniform. He looked as though he had been snatched from the battlefield and placed there, wounds still gaping and dripping with blood.

She had screamed and jumped from her bed, waking her roommate at the boarding house. Ruby's attempts to calm her failed, and Lorena wept uncontrollably on her shoulder. Hours afterwards, with Ruby resettled and snoring, she had lain awake until dawn staring at the flickering shadows on the ceiling cast from a tree outside her window against the moonlight.

The *Halifax II* slowed its speed in anticipation of a full stop at the boarding platform, jarring Lorena from her thoughts. The steam from its tall stack shot black smoke into the air, marring an otherwise perfect early morning sky. The snickering of horses, creaking of carts and chattering of passengers fell to the background as the city neared and the sounds of workmen with large equipment grew louder. The passengers grew restless, anticipating their arrival, and moved towards the exits.

Lorena held back, scanning the dock for familiar faces amongst the workmen, sailors and soldiers. There were many and they moved quickly, their minds on work. She felt the gentle thump of the ferry touching the dock, and her search became frantic. Where was he? Perhaps he had the day off, was on an errand or had already passed and was on his way to his ship. She was certain the ferry was on time, and he seldom left the dock without saying good morning.

She caught site of a sailor watching her from the shore and recognised him. It was Harry, a stoker on *Musquash*, the RCN minesweeping trawler at the dry dock wharf. He was the shipmate to the man she searched for. Harry watched her with a smile. Lorena hoped her Andrew was nearby and searched to the left and right of Harry. Her heart leapt when she spotted the blond-haired sailor in his blue uniform trimmed with white. His back was to her, and he was talking to two other men, his hands moving as he spoke. Her breath caught in her throat, and she pressed her fingers against the window. He had waited for her.

The squeaking of gates opening to let passengers and carts disembark reminded her she was in Halifax and needed to follow the crowd. Still, she waited, hoping Andrew would turn and see her. He touched Harry's shoulder and spoke to him, and Harry pointed at the ferry. Andrew turned, searched the windows of the ferry, then found her. He smiled and waved. Her body warmed and her smile broadened. She returned the wave, then sprang into action.

For what seemed an eternity, she lost sight of Andrew while

she joined the passengers to leave the ship and walk the ramp to the shore. She wished the people moved faster, but they trudged along at their Wednesday-morning pace. Directing herself to the edge of the crowd, she moved in the direction she had last seen Andrew. She knew he'd wait for her as he had done dozens of mornings before to give her a kind word and a smile. Since they had met one evening last week for supper, he had added a warm hug and a quick peck on the cheek to the morning greeting. Remembering the poem he had written for her that rested in her pocket, she recalled a few of the words he wrote: *Lovely as the wisps of clouds in a deep blue sky, with a contagious smile and twinkling eyes.*

Her white veil bounced in the wind from her quick steps that did not slacken until she spotted Andrew, who stood slightly taller than the other sailors around him did. Her heart beat against her chest and her hands warmed with anticipation.

"My little bluebird," Andrew said in a jovial voice. He scooped her into his arms, gave her a prolonged hug and kissed her cheek, lingering a little longer on her skin than the days previous.

Lorena held him fast, smelling the saltiness of his uniform and feeling the heat from his body. Her nerves tingled and for a second, her thoughts turned to lust. When they separated, the sparkle in his eyes enticed her to hold onto his hand. He squeezed it and stood shoulder to shoulder with her.

"The air is thick this morning," Andrew said. "Crisp and wily." He chuckled and winked at her.

The heat in her cheeks rose. "In deed it is, Able Seaman Pyke."

"Such formalities, Nursing Sister Brody."

"As a proper lady should promote." She returned the squeeze to his hand. She glanced at the other men in the circle. Harry stood straight, this hands clasped. When she caught his eye, he looked away. Next to him was Keith. She didn't know his title or last name. He was from Australia—she had discovered after asking about his accent—and served aboard HMCS *Niobe*. The man, only nineteen, had moved to Nova Scotia with his family when he was ten. The last sailor in the group was a stranger.

"Oooh." Keith slapped Andrew's shoulder. "It is right we're

here to chaperone, mate."

Lorena avoided Keith's gaze. There was no chaperone when she and Andrew had met the week earlier, and they had done things she'd never done before with a man. His hot kisses indicated he wanted to do more, but she held his hands as they attempted to explore her body. He did not press her and gently hugged her instead. She saw Harry watching her and again, he looked away, unamused by the comments.

"Although I'd love to dawdle longer, my bluebird," Andrew said, "we are expected on ship at 0800 hours this morning." He drew her near and whispered in her ear. "Tonight? Supper?"

She swallowed hard. Her parents would forbid her, but they were hours away in Pictou. No one but her landlord would know, and the middle-aged lady had enough to keep her busy with the boarding house and her three kids while her husband was overseas fighting the Germans. "Yes," she whispered.

"Wait for me here?"

"Same time?"

"Yes."

"Are we invited?" Keith chuckled.

Andrew grinned. "The invitation was not for you, Able Seaman, as you are not the prettiest woman on this dock."

Lorena's heart took flight. He thought she was pretty. But she wasn't. Her nose was slightly larger than those of other girls, and her hair was thick, heavy and dark, unlike the blondes she saw many sailors chase.

"You've embarrassed her," said the stranger in the circle sarcastically.

She looked for a safe place to anchor her gaze. It fell upon Harry who cast an unease expression.

Harry cleared his throat. "We don't want to be late for duty." His face lit up and he tried to rein in his smile. "Miss Brody, please excuse us."

"Of course," she said. "I do not wish for anyone to get into trouble."

Andrew rolled his eyes. "Fear not, young maiden. We shall

march double time to ensure we arrive as ordered." He leant near her ear. "See you this evening." He kissed her cheek, then walked away with a skip in his step, talking loudly with the others.

She watched him go, admiring his lean physic. Placing her hand on her cheek, she found it still moist from his lips. Harry's movement caught her attention as he looked back and gave her a subtle smile and nod. Then he faced forward and the four sailors disappeared into the crowd on the waterfront.

The smells in the operating room overwhelmed Lorena and although she wanted to be excused, she did not dare ask permission. The scorn of her father, who had pressured his political friends to get her into the nursing program, would be felt if she failed. He was not one to accept anything but the best from his children. After all, he had built his mercantile business from scratch, suffering great hardships to live the comfortable life he now lived.

Still, being a nursing sister wasn't what she dreamt of as her lot in life. Yet her father thought she was a natural as she tended to and healed the many animals on their farm. He could not understand treating animals was different from treating humans. She preferred teaching children, a vocation she had enjoyed for four years as she waited to reach the minimum entrance age of 21 for the nursing program. She reveled in expanding the minds of the young, teaching them about all the wonders of the world and reading books on fascinating subjects.

"Hold this."

The nurse shoved a pan into Lorena's hand and went to the nearby cupboard. Lorena held the pan steady as the doctor extracted the bullet and dropped it inside. This afternoon's exercise was shadowing an experienced nurse as Dr. Blume operated on a patient. It was a simple procedure: the removal of a bullet from the thigh. The young soldier was accidentally shot while his army mate had been cleaning his rifle. A *simple procedure* still involved blood, cutting into skin and sewing up the wound. In Lorena's eyes, this was not simple.

For the next 30 minutes, she did as instructed, moving about the room as if her mind was not the one controlling her actions. She attempted to keep her distance, to forget it was blood splattered on her white apron and to imagine the smell of it was nothing more than a noxious substance from the harbour, spewed from one of the many vessels coming and going. When she was instructed to clean the operation wound—a task she'd done many times—the familiar nauseas feeling resurfaced. She dabbed the stitched area with large wads of damp cloth, hoping to clean up quickly and leave to grab a quick breath of fresh air. However, when she was done, the nurse ordered her to wheel the patient to the recovery ward and to see to his needs.

Lorena silently followed the instructions and made the young soldier as comfortable as she could in the ward with a dozen other men. She glanced at the clock on the wall: 4:35. It was almost time to leave. She breathed a sigh of relief and her mind wandered to Andrew and their evening meal together. In other circumstances, she'd have requested time to return to the boarding home to freshen up before accompanying a gentleman to supper, but she did not want to lose the opportunity to spend time with Andrew. She'd have to be satisfied with tidying herself in the hospital's facilities before catching the tram to the ferry dock.

When the replacement nursing student arrived, Lorena made a few comments about the weather, then excused herself. Once in the washroom, she relieved her head of the white veil and tried to add life to her hair by drawing her fingers through it. The mirror told her it was futile, but she splashed water on her flattened locks and tried again. Within minutes, she was rushing out the front door and jumping onto the trolley headed for the waterfront. The jovial spirits of those on the trolley lifted hers, and she forgot about the dank smell in the operating room and the horrid sights she'd seen. Her Andrew was waiting for her near the ferry. Soon, her hand would be in his and they'd walk together as a couple. She giggled. They were a couple.

As the trolley ground to a stop, Lorena hopped off and with carefree steps, walked towards the waterfront. Several small groups chatted together beneath oil lights waiting for the ferry.

She'd be in one of those groups if not for Andrew. Strong arms wrapped around her from behind, and she squealed.

"Good evening, my little bluebird." Andrew rested his chin on her shoulder and looked into her eyes.

Lorena giggled and pressed against him. She felt the heat of his body through her overcoat and it ignited a fire that warmed her limbs. "Able Seaman Andrew Pyke, you startled me."

He laughed in her ear, then spun her around. "It's just Andrew tonight." He leant forward and snatched a kiss from her lips. "Mmm, Lorena, you taste better than any food I've eaten."

She smiled and looked away, the butterflies in her tummy taking flight. "Andrew," she scolded softly, "what will people say?" Though she knew she should release him, she didn't.

"I think they'd say, 'Look at that lovely couple; they're in love.' And I'd agree with them."

He drew her so close to his body, she felt his muscles. She gasped, and she pushed the warnings from her friend Ruby from her mind. Her roommate had cautioned her about sailors on the waterfront looking for only *one thing* and once they got it, they were off to the next girl or for overseas. Andrew wasn't like that.

"Are you hungry?" he asked.

"Famished."

"Then I shall keep you waiting no longer." He released her and held out his arm.

She hooked her arm with his and followed where he led. They walked past several noisy taverns before they arrived at a cosy restaurant. He took her overcoat and held the chair out for her. Her mother had told her it was a sign of a true gentleman.

"What does your heart desire tonight?" Andrew said as he settled into his chair.

Her first thought was *you*, but she dared not say it. Instead, she said, "A bowl of warm chowder. It will keep me warm for my walk home."

"I can warm you faster than chowder." He smirked and clasped her hands.

"Andrew." She patted his hand in reprimand but smiled as the thought of them together brushed her mind.

"See, I already warm your heart." He kissed her fingers.

The waitress came, took their order and before much time passed, served their meal. Lorena picked at her chowder, consuming it slowly as a young lady should in the company of a gentleman, though she wanted to gulp it down to fill her empty belly.

When the meal was done, Andrew walked her slowly back to the ferry. When they were halfway there, he sat her on a wooden bench beneath a street light and sat next to her.

"I have a surprise for you," he said, withdrawing a piece of paper from his pocket.

"Is it another poem?" Her hands covered her mouth. He truly loved her to go through the labour of writing poetry for her.

He cleared his throat and read the poem in a soft voice. He ended with, "Though the kiss of the dew may be sweet, it doth not compare to the sweetness of your smile." He folded the paper and handed it to her.

Lorena wanted to hop and sing and tell the world about the wonderful man who had entered her life. He was the man she had dreamt about while working long hours on her parents' farm, while she toiled away at nursing school. If she married him, she could avoid the gore of wounded soldiers and raise their family safely away from the horrors of war. She flung her arms around his neck and kissed him. He returned the kiss and drew her near. She felt his hand unfasten a button and slip beneath her coat. His caresses made her want him more, but she fought against the urge to surrender. Forcing them apart, she took a deep breath and refastened her button.

"Andrew, please understand. I must wait until my wedding night." She giggled but when she saw him frowning, she fell silent. "You do respect my wishes, don't you?"

"Of course." He forced a weak smile. "It's just that, I thought we had something special."

"We do!" She grasped his hand. "This is special."

"I know, but...we live in uncertain times. I will be called

overseas any day now, and I might not make it back."

"Don't talk such nonsense. You will come home. You have to. I'll be waiting for you."

"I know you will, and it makes me happy to hear you say that, but..." He looked off at the lights on the water. "So many men have gone and not returned."

"Rubbish. You will come home to me." She held his chin and turned him to look at her. "You're in my prayers, and I won't rest until you return."

He smiled and kissed her.

They walked hand-in-hand to the ferry where he kissed her again and waved as she boarded. As the ferry left the dock, she watched him walk away, his head down. Sadness swept over her. He wanted comfort from her, and she refused to provide it. A little kiss and cuddles wouldn't have harmed anyone. She admonished herself. She would make a horrible wife and a nurse, as she didn't know how to give anyone proper care. Andrew was right; he could be killed and his last memory of her would be a scolding. By the time she reached the Dartmouth shore, she promised herself she would make up the error in judgement when she saw him in the morning. This incident could not come between them and jeopardize their future together.

Lorena's head hurt. She had tossed and turned all night and when she finally fell into a deep sleep, it was in the wee hours of the morning. This made her sleep an hour past her usual wake up time. She rushed frantically, but she still missed the ferry by 30 minutes. As the *Halifax II* chugged off from Dartmouth, she was a solid hour behind schedule. Her heart sank. She was not there when Andrew passed this morning. Cringing, she wondered what message this had sent to him. He might think she was mad at him. She could not bear the thought of this and knew she had to rectify it before she attended the lectures.

Her thoughts compelled the ferry to go faster, but there was heavy traffic in the harbour this morning. A low murmur from the opposite side of the cabin interrupted her thoughts as she peered out the window at the Halifax shoreline. The ferry was too far away to make out individual people.

"That's a lot of smoke."

Lorena turned and strained her neck to see the smoke.

"I knew they'd hit," said an older man. "Impossible to quickly manoeuvre a vessel that large."

In the distance, a cloud of thick, black smoke rose from a large ship passing through the Narrows. It was moving away from the ferry, heading towards the Bedford Basin.

Lorena watched for a moment. The passengers' excitement rose as the smoke and flames did, but she did not feel the same enthusiasm. If men were injured on the burning ship, she might well be treating them later this morning. The thoughts of burn victims made an icy chill race down her spine. She had treated a few patients with burns and compared to other injuries, they were the ones she feared most. Shaking the feeling from her shoulders, she returned her gaze to the Halifax waterfront, hoping against all possibilities Andrew would be waiting for her.

A violent force from behind threw her against the window frame and she crumbled to the floor. Debris struck her, then fell from the ceiling. The shock stunned her for several moments. Screams pierced her ears, and she struggled to regain her balance and to stand. Her hands fell upon sharp objects, and she winced in pain. Opening her eyes, she saw glass covering the floor and blood dripping from her hands. The window she had stared out of was gone, exposing her to the cold December air of the harbour.

"Help me!"

Lorena turned to find a woman pinned beneath a bench. How she managed to get under there was beyond reason. She watched two men rush forward, grab onto the woman's arm and leg and pull her out.

"Is the ship sinking?" cried another woman, clinging to her young child.

"No." The man in the army uniform sounded unconvincing. "We'll make it to shore. Remain calm." He left, running up the stairs to the captain's house.

The same woman screamed and when Lorena looked, she

found her pointing at the window on the opposite side of the ship. Lorena looked past her and saw a huge wave heading for the ferry. It travelled so fast, she barely had time to draw a breath before it was upon them and splashing through the broken windows.

The frigid water stole Lorena's breath and she thrashed about, grabbing for a part of the ferry to secure herself. The water receded as quickly as it had come, and the woman who had screamed and her child were gone. Several men rushed to the open window and called for her, but no answer came.

Lorena stumbled forward, slipping on thick, black oil. She realised she was covered in the substance and so were the others. Holding onto a window frame, she stared at the bleak scene before her. What was once a beautiful shoreline filled with the activity of business was now a blackened landscape with smoke and flames. The once pristine water was inundated with debris and black oil. It rushed by as the ferry continued to sail towards Halifax. Long minutes passed as she surveyed the ships along the shore. She recognised the *Niobe*. It looked battered and the top looked heavily damaged. She strained to see the *Musquash* and saw light grey puffs of smoke rising from the deck.

A large lump froze in her throat. *Andrew*. Tears slipped down her cheeks and any effort to remove them only resulted in stings from oil pushed into her eyes.

Once the ferry reached the shore and the gates opened, she ran from the ship with the stream of people. Her thoughts were only on Andrew. Was he hurt? Did he think she was mad at him? Was he...? She couldn't finish the thought. Focussed on her task, she covered the ground between the ferry and the *Musquash* faster than she thought possible. She raced up the gangplank and bumped into a sailor on the way down. His face was covered in blood.

"Do you need help?" Lorena asked.

He shook his head and kept running.

She continued to the deck of the ship where she found several sailors attempting to put out a fire. Andrew was not amongst them. Not wanting to disturb them, she ran to the bow of the ship to see if she could find him. "Andrew! Are you here?"

A voice called out, and she searched the deck for its source. "Andrew? Where are you?" He called again, but she could not decipher the words. She ran in the direction in which she thought the voice came and saw a sailor pinned beneath a large metal object. Both the object and the sailor were covered with oil and dirt. She fell to her knees beside his head. "Andrew?" When he looked up at her, she knew it was not him for this man's eyes were brown not blue.

"Miss Brody could you please render..."—he struggled to speak and gulped air before continuing—"render service and help get this off me?"

The voice sounded familiar. "Harry? Is that you?"

"Yes, Ma'am."

Lorena scanned the piece of equipment as she stood. It looked heavy. She grasped the side and with a slippery grip tried to lift it. She managed to move it only slightly, then had to release it. Harry grunted. Footsteps made her turn. "Help me! Please."

The sailor stopped, gawked at her with wide eyes and stood frozen in place. He was injured and wore the filth of the explosion yet appeared capable of helping her. A familiar sparkle in his eyes triggered a memory.

"Andrew?" She ran to him and threw her arms around him. "It's you. You're alive."

"Lorena." He pushed her away. "We have to leave ship. It's going to blow!" He stepped away. "Let's go."

"We can't. Harry." She pointed to the sailor pinned beneath the equipment. "Help me get him free and then we'll leave together."

He shook his head wildly. "We have to go now!"

"We can't leave him here to die."

"We're all going to die." He turned and ran towards the gangplank.

Lorena watched him go, her mouth hanging open as he abandoned ship and shipmate. She turned back to Harry and stared at the heavy piece of equipment weighing him down. She needed help to get it off or...

"Miss Brody, if the ship is to explode, it is in your best interest to escape. Follow Andrew."

Lorena stood her ground. She could not leave this man to die. "I'll think of something." Her memories flashed back to her father as he raised a large stone from its place in the garden. He had used a large pole braced against a log. She saw a metal pole and grabbed it. The oily pole slid in her hand, but she managed to slide it over a steel box and wedge it under the equipment. With all her strength and weight, she lay upon the pole and the heavy piece of equipment rose.

"Wiggle out, Harry. Quickly."

Harry pulled himself free and pushed himself to his feet. He staggered and fell forward, but Lorena caught him before he dropped to the deck.

"Easy. Go slow." She cringed at the injury to his right shoulder. The open wound revealed a thick layer of flesh. "Stand still." She pulled off her nursing veil and realised it was too filthy to act as a sling. She unbuttoned her coat and removed her apron. The white material was soiled, but it was not saturated in oil. She fashioned it to hold his arm in place. "That will have to do until I can get you to the hospital."

"If there's a hospital left." He scanned the shoreline. "Everything is damaged."

"There will be a facility to tend to patients." Why she said that and where the hope came from, she didn't know. She positioned his left arm across her shoulder and they slowly walked towards the gangplank. Thankfully, Harry was a small man and when he stumbled, she was able to keep him upright.

"You should run to safety, Miss Brody." He coughed and gasped for air. "I'm slowing you down. I can make my own way."

"Nonsense." She lowered her brow and shot him a stern glance. "I could never leave you here in your condition." She remembered Andrew's quick exit, and uneasiness settled in her stomach. Not only had he abandoned his shipmate, he had left her. She had learned about shock and those who suffered from it, but it didn't forgive his actions. "Easy." She adjusted Harry's arm as they stumbled down the gangplank.

Several sailors rushed towards the ship and stopped at the bottom of the gangplank. Several others were casting off lines as if they were preparing to sail.

"Hurry!" shouted one. "We have to get this ship out of here before it blows."

Lorena quickened her pace. Why were these sailors rushing aboard, rushing into danger? Once on the dock, a sailor stopped to give Harry a quick assessment.

"Take him to Pier 4," said the sailor. "The *Old Colony* is serving as an emergency hospital." He rushed up the gangplank behind his shipmates.

Lorena stared at him as he raced towards danger. "If the ship is going to explode, why are they going onboard?"

"They need to get it out of here," Harry said. "If it explodes at the dock, it will kill more people."

"But the sailors will die." She stared into his brown eyes.

"This is what we signed up for. Our duty is to protect civilians." He nodded towards the dock where a dozen men worked frantically to release the ropes securing the *Musquash*. "We should get out of their way."

Lorena propelled herself forward, taking care not to slip on the slick surface. She was unsure of where to go until Harry pointed her in the right direction. They wove around debris scattered on the dock and frantic survivors as they searched for loved ones or ran to escape the horrors they witnessed. When they came upon a man covered in oil and lying still, she stopped. "Is he...?"

Harry leant down and shook the man, but he did not respond.

Lorena felt for a pulse and found none. She shook her head and an uneasy feeling rose into her throat. Though she had seen bodies taken to the morgue, she'd never touched one before.

"Let's keep going." Harry urged her to walk on.

Grasping onto the injured sailor, she stumbled forward, wishing away the thoughts invading her mind. She had seen too many people killed today. A large lump floating on the soiled water caught her attention. Through the smoke, she thought she saw movement and she pointed it out to Harry.

"I think he's drowned," he said.

"He moved his hand."

"It's probably the waves."

She walked slower and spied on the body floating on a tattered barrel twenty feet from shore. The man's hand moved again, and he raised his head slightly before it fell forward. "He's alive!" She directed Harry to the edge of the dock. "Hello!" she hollered. "Can you hear me?"

For a long moment, there was no movement, then a weak voice called out. "Aye."

"We have to save him." She searched the dock and found a length of rope. After balling it up, she threw one end to the man. It splashed into the water near him and drifted away slowly. "Grab the rope! Hey, mister, grab the rope."

He lifted his hand from the water but otherwise didn't move.

Harry stepped forward. "He's too weak."

Lorena watched in horror as the man slipped from the barrel and disappeared beneath the water. She threw off her coat, and Harry grabbed her arm.

"You can't." His eyes pleaded with her. "You'll not make it."

"With your help, I will." She shoved the rope into his hands. "When I get him, pull us ashore." She dove into the water, aiming for the spot she last saw the man. The icy water gripped her, making her want to escape to safety. In the early fall morning with thick clouds of smoke obscuring the sun and debris scattered about, the water looked murky and sinister. She latched onto a large shadow only to find it was an empty coat. When she saw a larger mass, she grabbed it; it was him. She fought to drag the man to the surface. Long before she reached fresh air, she thought her lungs would burst. Tears formed and disappeared in the salty harbour. When she broke the surface, she gasped for air and almost forgot she held onto a drowning man.

"Lorena! Grab the rope!"

Harry's voice brought her to her senses, and she searched

for the lifeline. After wrapping her arm under the chin of the man, she swam to it. Her limbs ached from the strain and the icy water. She latched onto the rope and held it with all her might. She moved forward and looked up to see Harry dragging the rope with his good arm.

"Don't let go!" he cried. "Please don't let go."

She held fast, praying to be out of the water soon. The frigid temperature bit at her flesh and when she bumped into a large piece of wood, she feared she'd lose her grip on the rope.

"You're almost there!" shouted Harry. "Hold on. I almost have you."

Through foggy eyes, she watched the dock grow nearer. Harry was directing her to a ladder. With the tide high, she was only four feet down from the top of the dock. When she bumped into it, a lightning rod of pain shot through her and she lost her grip on the rope. She thrashed about until she felt a force steady her. She looked to find Harry holding onto the jacket of the man.

"I'll drag him up. Let him go and hold onto the ladder."

She released the man and clung to the wooden rungs encrusted with seaweed, oil and dirt. Her mind drifted and pain beckoned her to sleep. The cold wind off the water blew into her face, making her close her eyes. The rhythm of the water rocked her, and she travelled home to the green fields of summers in Pictou. It relaxed her muscles and soothed her mind. Her fingers released the cold wood, and she plunged into the water. Her dip was short lived. A strong hand drew her upward and held her firmly.

"Lorena! Lorena!"

She opened her eyes and stared at Harry. He had somehow climbed down the ladder, wrapped his legs around the rungs and dragged her from the harbour. She clung to him, pressing her face against his neck.

"Hold onto the ladder." He squeezed her tightly. "You have to climb up."

"And you?"

"I'll be right behind you."

She hesitated to release him, but she couldn't stay here. With frozen fingers, she grasped the rungs.

"Go slow," he said. "You can do it. You're an amazing woman."

His dark eyes swept over her face, and she saw an emotion she'd never before seen in a man who gazed at her.

"Over here!"

Lorena looked up at the sound of voices, and a soldier's head popped over the side of the dock.

"Two more over here," he said, and waved to someone behind him. He fell to his knees and reached out a hand. "Miss, let me help."

She grasped the hand, and the strong man pulled her to safety. "Harry." She pointed at the ladder. "Help him. He's injured." One of the four men came to her and wrapped her coat around her. Within seconds, Harry was on the dock and gathering her in his good arm. She pressed against him, thankful to be alive.

"He's breathing." One of the soldiers had checked the man who had almost drowned. "But he needs medical attention quick."

Lorena examined him, searching for serious injuries. He wore a sailor's uniform, but he was missing his hat and boots. One of their rescuers wiped his face with a rag, cleaning his mouth, nose and eyes of oil. She thought she recognised the face and peered closer. "It's Keith." She glanced at Harry. "It's Keith."

Harry twisted and leant towards the sailor. "You're right." He looked at the other men. "He's from the *Niobe*."

"He's headed for *Old Colony* now." The soldier ushered the man with the cart closer. "Let's get him loaded." Once Keith was in the cart, he reached for Lorena. "Let's go."

She reluctantly released Harry and allowed the man to lift her into the cart. Harry climbed in beside her and the horse began at a quick pace towards Pier 4.

Many hours later, scrubbed clean of oil and dirt and wearing a clean nursing uniform, Lorena leant against the wall to catch her breath and some sense of normalcy. When she had arrived onboard *Old Colony*, a change of clothes and a warm tea brought her body back to life, and she assisted the doctors as a steady stream of patients crossed their tables. It was nearing midnight, and she was told to go home or at least rest. She had no strength to make the walk to the ferry and to the boarding house, so she decided to remain on ship. She had checked on Keith and found him peacefully sleeping. The nurse tending to him said he'd recover with time. Now she sought to find the other man she had saved, one who had saved her in turn.

The noise level on the ship had reduced compared to the day's activities, but she still heard the moans of the dying and those in pain and the nurses and doctors still working feverishly to save them or to make them comfortable. She sneaked through the ship, not wanting to disturb anyone, peeking in doorways hoping to find Stoker Harry McEntire. When she did, she slipped inside his room and sat quietly in the chair next to his bed. He appeared to be sleeping but when she settled, she found him watching her. A gentle smile creased his lips.

"Stoker McEntire," she whispered. "You should be sleeping."

"Miss Brody, so should you."

She grinned. He had only ever called her that except when he was shouting to save her life. He had been there when Andrew... She struggled to understand the man who claimed to love her. Having time to think about what had happened, she knew he had abandoned her, left her there to die. She swallowed hard and tears welled.

"What's wrong?"

She dabbed her eyes and tried to fight the sadness. "Andrew."

"Is he okay?"

"Yes. I think so." She shrugged. "I don't know. I haven't seen him since this morning."

Harry watched silently for a long minute, then said, "You love him, don't you?"

"I thought I did." She sniffed and folded her arms across her

94

chest. "I thought he was a good man." She looked up quickly. "Good men get scared. Run. Do things they wouldn't normally do. Yes, that's what happened." She stared into the distant shadows as she thought about the past few weeks. The emotions Andrew had stirred excited and confused her.

She remembered the tattered paper wrapped in a rag in her pocket and withdrew it. "He's a lovely writer. He truly loves me, and I must understand the strain he was under." She flattened the paper Andrew had given her the night before. The water and oil made it impossible to read except for a few words. "A man would not write this if he didn't feel it." She traced the lines. "When I think of you, I think of...daisies..."—she strained to see the words—"my soul..." She sobbed. "I can't remember the words."

"When I think of you," Harry said softly, "I think of daisies dancing in the wind. My heart, my soul, my everything are all in a spin."

She looked up and eyed him. "Andrew showed you the poem?"

He stared at his hands and in a low voice said, "I wrote it."

"You what?"

He cleared his throat and gazed at her with sullen eyes. "I wrote it. I wrote the first one too." He winced. "At first, I didn't know it was for you. I thought it was for another woman he bragged about."

"So these poems were not about me?" Her heart sank.

He released a sigh. "They were...I—I wrote how I felt, and he gave them to you." He looked away, cautiously glancing at her.

"Stoker Harry McEntire, how could you deceive me like this?"

"Please forgive me. When I learned he gave the poem to you, I should have spoken up, but you"—he closed his eyes for a moment as if to absorb pain—"were so happy, and I could tell you liked him."

"Is this how you truly feel?" Lorena held up the soiled paper.

He glanced at it, then at her and nodded.

"Do you remember the poem?"

"I do."

"Then you can rewrite it for me?"

He nodded.

"And sign your name to it?"

Puzzled, he studied her. "I can."

"Good." She dried her eyes, crumpled the paper and shoved it into her pocket. "Able Seaman Pyke has a lot of explaining to do when I next see him." She leant forward and pulled the blankets up to Harry's chin. "Stay warm." She fluffed his pillow. "Is there anything you need?"

He shook his head.

"Now get your rest. It will help you heal." She retrieved a blanket from a nearby cupboard and resettled in the chair. "I'll be here if you need me." She yawned. "As a nursing sister." She smiled. "And when you are well, we'll talk about the contents of those poems." His face lit up.

"Yes, ma'am."

∾

Bronwen Piper

Since Bronwen Piper was sixteen, she's scribbled on napkins, the back of envelopes that arrive in the mail and brown paper bags. She takes these scraps, organises them on her floor and creates stories from them. She is the author of the upcoming *The Road We Travel*, the first book in The Journey series.

She enjoys reading cosy mysteries under a warm blanket with a dish of chocolate nearby.

Forever Green

Barbara-Jean Moxsom

Halifax, Nova Scotia, 1992

CATHY HOULAHAN ARRIVED AT CAMP Hill Hospital an hour before her scheduled shift. She needed the extra time to prepare for the long day ahead. Nursing proved to be more difficult than she had imagined. And imagination, Cathy had learned, needed to be more practical and less fantastical.

Helping people had always been her passion. She loved to be useful and gained a great deal of pleasure knowing in some small way, she improved someone's life. But doubt had loomed overhead since last week's discussion with the hospital's chief of staff, Alex Griffen. Walking out of the meeting left her perplexed. Rules, regulations and standard operating procedures were sobering to an idealist. She had always been a dreamer, living on high hopes and believing in infinite possibilities. She naively assumed the best in people and was a willing and eager participant in life's great adventures.

Despite Cathy's past disappointments, she remained true to who she was: a caring, hopeful optimist.

This meeting with Alex reminded her of another eye-opening experience. Her 'age of reason' happened before she turned eighteen when her childhood sweetheart, Darren MacPherson, moved away. It took a long time before she realised her teenage years had been centred around her dream of their future together. Like Romeo, Cathy was in love with the idea of being in love. She knew she had to step down from the clouds if she wanted to walk on solid ground. She thought she had tamed her spirit. She focussed her attention on an education and was fortunate to find a job soon after she graduated. Three years working the wards gave her confidence to apply for the opening in the palliative care unit. But somehow, the dreamer had re-emerged.

Alex bluntly pointed that out. His matter-of-fact mannerism reminded her of a professor at Dalhousie University who used to say, 'Life happens, and then we die. Death is natural; it's a part of life.'

And now again, Cathy had been warned of the first rule of nursing: do not allow yourself to become attached to the patients, especially those in the palliative care unit. Be personable, not personal. This was a mandate much easier said than done and difficult to self-monitor.

Cathy greeted staff members along the corridors while she made her way to the hospital's chapel. Sitting in the front pew, she removed her jacket, pulled her binder from her over-sized bag and skimmed through the pages. Pharmaceutical companies were continuously manufacturing new medication, and she liked to be well-versed on them. It aggravated her when they discontinued a product that benefited her patients. She believed greed played a part in the process. The 'new and improved' medicines tended to cost more and come with additional side-affects.

Cathy turned her attention to her patients. Her first thoughts went to Donald whose cancer had progressed rapidly. She hoped his family would arrive soon. Driving across country in late November could be treacherous. Molly refused to take her heart medication, and dear old Sam kept holding on waiting for his son to visit.

Cathy knew all their stories. These patients were more than a simple bed number. They were people who once had dreams of their own. She also considered the possibility that one day, she might be a patient in a hospital somewhere. And when, or if that day came, she hoped the nurses would treat her with respect and allow her dignity.

She couldn't help listening to details when patients were irate, in pain or lonely. It was personal. Yet she knew her duties came first. She was mindful of her actions and reactions. She kept it professional and demonstrated patience with her patients.

But in the chapel, she found a quiet, safe place to unload. Call it therapy. Call it prayer. It didn't matter. She discovered when her mind was thinking and wandering, there was no better place to reflect and unleash the multitude of emotions, complaints and criticisms than a private space where she felt safe to think the thoughts she was told not to think. Once her mind was cleared, she could focus on her work.

Cathy checked her watch: 4:40 pm. She put away her binder, grabbed her jacket and stood to leave. Looking up at the simple wooden cross, she spoke quietly. "Well, God, those are my thoughts for today. I hope you can make sense of it. I gotta get to my station. Thanks for listening."

Before she reached the door, she turned back to make a few requests. "Hey, do you suppose you could help Mary sleep tonight? She gets cantankerous. Maybe you could ask Miss Roselyn to drop her duchess attitude; I really can't handle that. If she held any title in my books, it would be Miss Royal Pain in My Ass! And I'm tired of Ross' sick sense of humour. He's a pervert who disgusts me. Either heal him or take him home with you 'cause I can't tolerate him anymore. And finally, can you give me strength to be cheerful when I tend to Sam. The last thing he needs is my pity."

Hearing those words aloud brought tears to her eyes. She took a deep breath, closed her eyes and slowly exhaled before leaving the chapel.

The nurse's station was abuzz when Cathy arrived. "What's going on?" she asked.

"We're organizing a Christmas Carole," Pauline said.

"I can't believe tomorrow is the first day of December," Nancy said. "Ya know we could start decorating at the stroke of midnight."

"I don't think anyone would appreciate us lugging decorations

99

around while they're trying to sleep," Cathy said. "Let's wait until morning. Has anyone done their rounds?"

"We just got here," Pauline said. "We haven't had a chance to review the charts yet."

"All right. Let's put this away and look at it during break," Nancy said.

Cathy scanned the desk. "Are there any messages?"

"Nope," Nancy said. "But I see flowers! Aren't they gorgeous!"

"The front desk gave them to me when I arrived," Pauline said. "They're for Sam. I figured Cathy would want to deliver them." She winked. "After all, she did pay for them."

"Why would you say that?" Cathy asked.

"It's no secret how much you admire him. And we all know his son is too thoughtless to do anything like this. Where did you get them?"

"I'm not telling."

"Don't you think this falls under personal attention?" Pauline asked.

"What I do on my own time is my business." Cathy took the vase of flowers and headed down the hall.

"Ooh, sassy!" Nancy chuckled. "Tell Sam we said hello."

Cathy entered the room holding the flowers in front of her face, hoping to surprise Sam by doing her best Oprah operatic impression. "I have a special delivery for someone." The room was quiet. She peeked from around the bouquet and saw the hospital bed was empty.

"He's gone," a voice said.

She turned to see Bed B was occupied. Stunned, she averted her attention to the flowers. Then she glanced at the bedside table to see if the decorative ceramic handle was on the drawer, the handle that was brought up in her meeting with Alex. Cathy had explained, 'Sam had a small yet poignant request; he wanted a hint of his wife's décor in the room.' And there it was. White porcelain with blue roses; confirmation she had entered the right room.

"Psst!" came an insistent voice from the hallway. She looked to find Nancy and Pauline waving their arms at her. Returning her attention to the flowers, she walked forward. "I'll set these on the window sill."

"Don't bother. I don't want them," said the man in Bed B. "Give them to someone who'll appreciate them?"

"Are you allergic to flowers?"

"No. They don't interest me."

Cathy hesitated. She was caught in a whirlwind of unexpected circumstances and confusion had taken over. Attempting to communicate while riding an emotional rollercoaster never fared well. Snap out of it, she told herself and made a decision. "I'll leave them here until I find someone who wants them?" She forced a cheerful tone. "I'll be back shortly." She left the room and followed Pauline and Nancy to the nurses' station.

"We just found out," said Pauline somberly.

"Sam went into cardiac arrest early this morning." Nancy placed a comforting arm across Cathy's shoulders. "The nurses couldn't revive him. They said he had a good night before it happened. It was fast."

Cathy barely had time to acknowledge the fact, when she saw a man in a trench coat storm towards the desk.

"Where is my father?" He looked at Cathy. "I want to see him." He appeared to be in his forties. He looked refined toting a briefcase, but his demeanour was pure arrogance.

Pauline intercepted him. "Keep your voice down, sir. Who are you looking for?"

"My name is Eric MacKenzie." He glared at her. "I am a lawyer, and I am looking for my father, Sam MacKenzie. Where is he? I was just in his room and he's not there."

"You should speak to his doctor," Pauline said. "I'm surprised he didn't contact you."

"He did," Eric said. "I received a call saying my father went into cardiac arrest." He stepped closer, resting his hand on the counter. "Where is his doctor? Dr. Flemming?"

Nancy grabbed a clipboard from the desk. "He's on duty

today. He'll be here in about ten minutes."

Before Eric spewed more demands, Cathy jumped in. "I'll take you to him." She walked away from the nurse's station unsure if Eric followed. She assumed he would. He didn't seem the type to be able to wait ten minutes. Sure enough, she saw his reflection on the elevator doors as she passed them. After rounding the corner at the end of the corridor, Cathy pulled open a door and stood, reluctantly awaiting Mr. MacKenzie's arrival.

Eric entered the room and, seeing it empty, asked, "Where's Flemming?"

Cathy shut the door and walked past him. "*Dr.* Fleming will be here in about ten minutes. Have a seat." She gestured to a bench and sat a safe distance away from it.

He sat and looked around. "What is this, a chapel?"

"I like to call it divine intervention." Cathy smiled. "Yelling out there is not appropriate. But in here, it is acceptable."

He stood. "I don't have time for this. Where is..."

"Sit down!" she ordered and was pleasantly surprised when he did. "Do you realise the pain you've inflicted on everyone? Not only your father but also all of us. For months, your father waited for you to visit, but you always had an excuse. We were the ones who picked up the pieces and dealt with his anguish. Every action, or lack thereof, has a consequence. I would come here to curse you every time you disappointed him." Reliving the pain fuelled her anger. "Everyone in this building from the doctors, to the nurses, the kitchen staff, the laundry crew, the night janitors, and even the maintenance crew respected your father. We all knew him. We took time to tend to his needs. So don't you dare bring your pompous ass in here and demand anything from us. You are the only one at fault." She stood. "I have patients to see. I'm on duty in two minutes. You can sit here and ask for forgiveness, which I highly doubt you will, or you can wander the halls while you wait for Dr. Flemming. I don't care. As a lawyer, you might have a worthy reputation but as a son, everyone in this place thinks you're a worthless piece of shit."

Before she reached the door, he spoke. "You're a bit late. Your friend already delivered this speech." He watched her expression.

102

"Don't look surprised. I'm a lawyer. I know when two people collaborate their stories. Well done."

"Excuse me?" she asked.

"The old man in my father's room tore a strip off me the minute I walked in. He wasn't as polite as you. Regardless, you both made valid points. You may not believe me, but I appreciate what you have done. Sometimes life gets in the way, you know."

"No. I see it as work getting in the way of life. Don't you realise, every choice we make affects someone? You may have created heaven for yourself but by doing so, you created hell for the rest of us." She abruptly turned and left the room, returning to her station a bundle of nerves. She picked up a chart, glanced at it, then put it down, knocking the phone off the base. Her fingers fumbled with the receiver before putting it back on the stand. She grabbed a pen, then tossed it down, asking, "What am I doing?"

"Cathy," Pauline said, "why don't you take a break?"

"We can cover for you," Nancy added.

Cathy exhaled. "Maybe I should. I can't focus. I just read that chart and I have no idea who it belongs to." She held her hand flat in the air to examine it; it trembled. "I can't believe I did that. I told him off. Oh my God, what have I done? I got too personal. Oh shit, he's a lawyer." Her eyes grew wide. "What if he sues me? What if he presses charges? I could lose my job over this!"

"Calm down," Nancy said. "What happened?"

"I took him to the chapel and I blasted him." She paused and smiled. "God it felt good!"

"You were in the chapel?" Pauline asked. "You can tell the judge you were confessing and he overheard it. Then you can sue him for publicly speaking about your private confession. See? Relax. You have nothing to worry about."

"You're right. Thank you. I'll be fine. I just need to…" The stranger in Bed B popped into her mind. "Who is in Sam's room?"

Nancy reached for his chart. "Timothy Richard Kennedy. He refused chemo and radiation once they opened him up and realised he was too far gone. Pancreas. He's in a lot of pain. He's on a morphine drip. Do you want me to tend to him?"

"No. I'll do it." She took the chart and walked down the hall. When she entered the room, she instinctively looked towards Sam's bed. A dry cough turned her attention to Bed B. "Good afternoon"—she glanced at the chart—"Timothy Richard Kennedy. How are you feeling? Are you comfortable?"

"Richmond," he said between coughs.

"Rich...?" Cathy pulled a pen from her pocket and made a note on the chart. "Timothy Rich-mond Kennedy."

"Timothy Richmond Green."

Green? She double-checked the impression of his medical card stamped in the corner of his chart. "According to your card, you are Timothy Richard Kennedy. That is the name I must put on your records."

"I prefer Green."

"All right. Is that a family name?"

"Nope. Just a preference."

"Fine. On paper, you will be Kennedy, but I will respectfully call you Mr. Green. Will that work for you, Mr. Green?"

"Yes."

"I see you have a birthday coming up on December 6th. That's less than a week away." She did the math, "You will be 82! Good for you."

"I don't celebrate my birthday," he said.

"That's too bad." She checked his morphine drip. "Religious reasons or a preference?"

"Let's not do this," he said. "We don't need to get personal. You bring me medicine and I'll keep my business to myself. How does that sound?"

"Boring but practical."

Pauline entered the room with a clipboard and a great deal of enthusiasm. "Hello, Mr. Kennedy, we're decorating this floor tomorrow. Do you have any objections to us putting lights or garland in here?"

"Yes, I do," he said sternly. "And the name's not Kennedy; it's Green. G-r-e-e-n. Green. The only decoration I want to see is a forty-foot tree in the middle of this room. Can you do that?"

Pauline stood frozen with a blank expression. "That's impossible," her energy faded when she realised he wasn't joking. "OK, understood, no decorations. Thank you." She turned slowly and left the room.

"Is there a remote for the TV?" Mr. Green asked.

"There should be." Cathy found it in the cubby of the TV's frame. "Here it is." After pushing the power button on, she saw nothing but static, a sign the TV was not hooked up to the cable. "Does your insurance cover the TV?"

He looked stunned by the question. "The TV is not free?"

She returned the remote to the cubby, crossed the floor to Sam's TV and angled it towards him. "This TV is paid in full until the end of December. It's yours as long as this bed stays vacant. How good is your eye sight?"

"Good," he said. "Let's hope the bed stays vacant."

"Do you want CTV News? There's *Live at 5*, then *Steve Murphy at 6:00*. What time is it?" She checked her watch. "5:15. Supper should be here soon." Cathy noticed his feet were partially exposed. "Do you want your feet covered?"

He nodded. "It's cold in here, and there's nothing to these blankets."

Cathy adjusted the blankets and noticed deep scars on the bottom of his left foot. "Ouch. What happened here?"

"Glass."

"Did you kick in a window?"

Noise rang out in the hall as meal carts rattled. The mixed aromas made their way into the room.

"Mmm, soup's on!" Cathy said. "Are you hungry?"

"A little bit," he admitted.

Cathy believed she was making headway with Mr. Green. Their conversation felt less tense and more natural.

The food attendant entered the room and set the tray on the rolling table beside the bed. He took a moment to adjust its position to be within reach. "Here ya go, Mr. Kennedy. Pork, mashed potatoes, green beans, a roll, apple sauce, a cup of tea and a glass of tomato juice. Enjoy." He smiled as if waiting for a tip.

"It's Green."

The man's smile quickly vanished. "Yes, sir, those are green beans. We'll serve yellow wax beans tomorrow night."

"I'm talking about my name. It's Mr. Green," he snapped.

The attendant turned a light shade of red. "My mistake, Mr. Green. It won't happen again." He turned and left the room.

Cathy watched Mr. Green lift off the lid and a cloud of steam billowed out from the food tray. "Don't you find pork a little heavy?"

"Not really. There's not much here."

"Very funny," she said. "So what's with the name Mr. Green?"

"The name Timothy feels foreign to me," he said reluctantly. "I never recognised it as my own. I associate it more with my brother. That's why I kept it. Richmond was the community I grew up in. And Green reminds me of an evergreen tree." He raised his brow. "Satisfied? Can I eat now?"

"Of course, I have other patients to see, but I'll be back to check on you later." She turned to leave but stopped when he spoke.

"You insisted on knowing my name, but you never bothered to tell me yours."

"Yes, I did." She paused to think. "I always introduce myself when I meet a new patient."

"You were too busy with the flowers."

She glanced at the flowers, and it triggered her memories. Guilt washed over her. She wanted to morn but policy insisted she perform her duties. "You're right. I was. My name is Cathy."

"I assumed so," he said. "You sounded like the gal Sam highly recommended."

"When were you admitted?" She glanced at his chart, and before he could answer, she said, "Saturday. I was off all weekend. So you spoke with Sam."

"Sometime when you're not busy, I'll tell you about our

weekend together."

"I look forward to hearing about it." Cathy hesitated. "After my shift." Later that evening, Cathy returned. Mr. Green genuinely appeared enthusiastic when she entered the room, but a TV commercial altered his mood. A documentary for the seventy-fifth anniversary of the Halifax Explosion was scheduled to air on Sunday December 6th. She recalled Mr. Green's birthday was the same day. He would be 82, which meant he would have been seven at the time of the tragedy.

"How much do you remember?" She asked while she checked his morphine drip.

"Too much," he said. "You don't forget something as devastating as that. And you never forget not having the chance to celebrate your seventh birthday. What are you doing? I thought you were off duty."

"I am. I guess old habits are hard to break." She chuckled as she sat in the chair. "I don't know anyone who witnessed the explosion. I couldn't imagine what it was like."

"That's the problem today. Everybody has it too easy. They can't appreciate anything if they don't have struggles. Try standing in line for three hours waiting for a bowl of soup, your only meal for the day."

"I've never experienced anything like that. Care to share?" His gaze fell to his hands that appeared to have seen a lot of work in their time, and she watched him struggle with his memories. Just when she felt he would tell her to leave, he spoke. His voice was low and uncertain.

"I was at school when the fire started."

"Your school was on fire?"

"No, the fire was in the harbour." He glanced up quickly, then back at his hands. "I was outside, hiding behind the school trying to decide if I was going to run away." He shook his head. "But it was so damn cold. I was crouched in a ball trying to keep warm. I didn't know where I was going to run to, so I figured I may as well go to school. The minute I stood up, I heard fire engines and sirens blaring." He paused and stared out the window into the dark night.

Cathy thought the pain of that moment would prevent him from continuing. "You didn't hear the explosion?"

"The explosion happened after the fire." He took a deep breath. "At first, all I saw was thick grey smoke coming from the harbour. I didn't know what was going on. I heard people yelling. You know, neighbours stepping out to get a better look hollering to each other. Then a wave struck me. It wasn't water; it was air or wind. It was like an invisible cloud, but I could see it." He looked at Cathy. "That's the only way I can describe it. It raced towards me. It was like looking through the bottom of a glass bottle. Imagine it as big as the harbour itself coming straight at you. There was no time to run. I got hit. My arms and legs flung forward as my body thrust up in the air. It was like the cartoons. I saw tree tops!"

"Oh my God!" Cathy gasped.

"Oh my God is right. He spared me that day." He cast a glance to the window again and stared for a moment at the darkness outside before continuing in a monotone voice. "I don't know how I survived." He pursed his lips and shook his head gently. "My wrist was broke. I must have passed out. I don't know. When I came to I didn't recognise anything." His voice cracked and he looked down at his hands.

Cathy was on the edge of her seat. The thought of a little boy facing those dangers and that bleak reality brought tears to her eyes. For a long moment, she thought Mr. Green would end the story there, but he cleared his throat and spoke again in a quieter tone.

"There was smoke. Thick smoke. Some places thicker than others. I walked where it was thin. Walking was hard. There was loose, uneven rubble everywhere. Nails stuck out of wood. There was so much glass. I shivered so bad my teeth chattered, but I couldn't hear them over the sirens and people screaming. I tried to get home to mother. My foot hurt. I looked down and saw I had lost a boot. I lost my coat and mittens, too. I looked for my boot, but it was useless. I broke down. I cried like a baby." He wiped a tear from his cheek. "Home. That's all I thought of.

I don't remember getting there. I just remember being there."

"Those scars on your foot are from walking on glass?" She patted his ankle gently. "I heard almost every window broke that day."

"Just about. What I have always found strange was everything was cloudy, fuzzy, yet so clear. Everything happened so fast, but I have glimpses as if it was slow motion. It was surreal, like living in a nightmare."

"What happened when you got home?"

"I found my house crushed. As if something slammed down on it. The foundation was intact, but the rest was a pile of rubble. I stood there and watched men digging their way through the wreckage. Every house on my block was gone. I heard someone call out my name. I looked around and saw a man running towards me. I thought it was my father. I figured he came home early from the sugar refinery. 'Timothy, are you all right?' he shouted." He nodded solemnly and blinked several times to stall the tears.

Cathy reached for the box of tissue on the bedside table and handed it to him. He set the box on his lap, pulled a tissue and quickly dabbed his eyes.

"It was my brother. I was relieved and confused at the same time. He never called me Timothy. I was Moth. 'Go away, Moth; you bug me,' he would say as he swatted his hand towards me. I thought he hated me. He tormented the hell out of me whenever he was bored. He was the reason I was going to run away. And now, he was the reason I was staying. 'Come on, little brother,' he said. 'Help me find mother.'" He took a deep breath. "We dug for hours. Just before dark, ladies came and brought the kids to the church basement for shelter. There was a blizzard that night. The wind and snow came through the boards they had put over the broken windows." Mr. Green reached for his water and sipped from a straw. His eyes appeared to be miles away.

"Were you able to reach your mother?"

He moistened his lips and dabbed his eyes again with the tissue. "A neighbour carried her out." A tear rolled freely down his cheek and he sniffled. "We laid her on a mattress. I saw her coat under our front door, so I grabbed it and tried to put it on her. I managed to get one arm in, but it was hard on account of my broken wrist. My brother—I never knew him to be so caring—put his hand on my shoulder and asked what I was doing. I told him it was cold; I wanted her to be warm." Tears streamed from his eyes. He snatched more tissue and blew his nose. "I'll never forget what he said. 'Timothy, Mother doesn't need it now, but she would want you to wear it. Put the coat on and I'll go find a blanket to put over her." His hands wiped his face as if washing away the pain. "Thousands died that day. I lost my sisters and my parents. All I had left was my brother. I find it incredible to think the one person I despised the most turned out to be the same person I most admire. He saved me that day. He was a good man, and I loved him."

"What was his name?"

"Fred. Frederick Allen Kennedy. The next morning, he took me to North Street Station. That was the old train station; it's not there anymore. He was a baggage handler. Word was people were coming to help. And let me tell ya, a ton of people came off the trains: doctors, nurses, construction workers, firemen. I couldn't believe how many people there were. They came from all over the world. Some as far as China! My uncle from Boston came too. He was my mother's youngest brother. He worked at a bank or an investment firm. He was twenty-two; hard to believe. He seemed so grown up. He was amazing."

"Tell me more about him," Cathy insisted.

"Around the 15th of the month, my uncle and I set out to find a tree. He had the idea that if we put an evergreen tree in parade square, it would brighten up people's spirits. We went to the Arm, that's the Armdale Rotary area. It was a long ride, but it was worth it. I stood amongst the trees in awe and cried. I never saw anything so beautiful. They were luscious and green. I used to call them Forever Green Trees." He chuckled. "Kids say the darnedest things. I looked at my uncle and saw he was wiping tears from his eyes, too. I told him his eyes looked happy." He smiled, showing Cathy a glimpse of the little boy who still resided inside. "Those trees brought us so much joy. I know that sounds silly, but you must understand; the colour had gone. The city was grey. Even the snow was grey. The sky was grey. Everything was charred or covered in dust. After we picked a tree for the square, I asked my uncle if we could get another tree for Boston. I figured he could take it with him when he was ready to leave. It could be a gift to show our thanks and appreciation for all they had done. He loved the idea and together we picked the biggest tree we could drag with our horses. That was a turning point for me. Seeing those trees brought hope back into my life. It gave me a reason to live."

"So you're the guy." She was blown away. "You're the guy who started the tradition."

"Yup," he said. "Me and Sam."

"Sam?" She was confused.

"Sam was my uncle."

"What? Sam was your uncle? Why didn't you tell me?"

"I'm sure I did."

"No, I would have remembered that."

"Huh. I told you we spent the weekend together."

"Yes."

"Did I tell you he wanted to see the harbour?"

"No." She was shocked.

He proudly announced, "I took him up on the roof. Well, me and the maintenance crew. But that's another story." He put the tissue box back on his bedside table and adjusted his blankets. "I'm tired. I think I'll turn in for the night."

Four days later, on December 4th, Cathy proudly walked into Mr. Green's room carrying what looked like a bouquet of flowers. "Good morning, Mr. Green."

"Hello, Cathy," he said, "What have you got there?"

"An early birthday present. A special delivery." She delicately unwrapped the potted balsam fir.

"Look at that; it's a Forever Green Tree!" His eyes lit up.

"Happy Birthday, Mr. Green. And if anyone asks, it didn't come from me."

∾

Barbara-Jean Moxsom

Barbara-Jean Moxsom, from Halifax, NS, began her career in advertising as a product illustrator before entering the printing industry as a graphic artist. A course in classical animation led to a studio in Halifax.

In 1999, now a stay-at-home mom, the real work began.

To date, Barb is a published illustrator (*I'm Not Stupid* by George Gasek), an award-winning cartoonist (Norton and Penny, On The Loose, and Gullivan's Travels), a playwright (*Next Big Star, Lost in the Boonies, Seniority Rules, Welcome to Corridornia, Mrs. O'lander's Brew* and *A Royal Heist*) and author (*Bible Lessons from Buddy*).

Neighbours

Liana Olive Quinn

THE SWEET SMELL OF BISCUITS baking permeated the air, overpowering the odour of burning wood in the cast iron stove. The aroma and cosy warmth filling the kitchen made it easy to forget the frost that clung to the windows in intricate designs and the wisps of wind that sneaked in through the crevices around the frames and doorway. December in Halifax shocked the system, telling the body winter was on the stoop and would enter with no further notice. Those who predicted the weather need not bother telling Bessie Tucker the skies above would soon crush the final breaths of fall; her bones aching with weariness and popping from movement foretold of an approaching storm. Given the recent temperatures, it would not be rain.

The quick snap as steam split wood inside the stove reminded her that the wood box was near empty. Her oldest son Angus had forgotten to replenish the spent wood the night before. His mind had been elsewhere, he had said, but she knew someone not somewhere had preoccupied it. The young girl he pined for was not to be trusted, and Bessie would see to it personally that Angus did not court the German *Fräulein*.

A heavy cart rumbled by, and Bessie scratched a peek hole in the frost and peered through the thick glass. She watched the milk wagon halt at the neighbour's home across the street. The Müllers conveniently changed their name to Miller shortly after the war had started in an attempted to hide their ethnic origin, but Bessie did not participate in the charade. When she saw Elisabeth *with an S* on the street, she bid her a good day by saying, "Lovely weather we're having, Mrs. Müller." The disarmed expression crossing the woman's face revealed her shame. Not once did Elisabeth ask Bessie to refrain from using her true name, which indicated in her heart, she was still German.

Bessie espied the middle-aged woman, dressed in layers of skirts and shawls to fend off the morning chill, chatting silently with the milkman. Bartering was more likely the conversation that went on out of Bessie's earshot. In the past, she had witnessed Elisabeth argue the price of wares until the vendor reduced it by a penny or more. She took advantage of Canadians' good nature, but the Hun received no kindness from the country's soldiers on the battlefield.

In the dim, grey morning, Elisabeth Müller, dressed in bland colours of light brown, tan, faded black and grey, could be passed easily without notice as she stood in front of the bleak colours of the house. Was this how the enemy hid from British troops, blending into the background as if they were not there? Bessie frowned. Germans were sneaky with little honour.

"Mother."

Shocked from her thoughts, she turned abruptly to find her oldest child standing fully dressed in the middle of the kitchen. "Angus, where do you think you're off to at this hour?"

"I was about to fetch the milk for you, dear Mother." His dark head motioned towards the door. "The wagon is here."

Her brow furrowed. "Mr. Burns will deliver to this side of the street shortly. We've plenty of milk to carry us through breakfast." She left the window. "While you're dressed for the cold, fetch me an armload of wood. You can fill the box after school."

She watched him struggle for words, then he lowered his head and shuffled out the back door. A brisk wind blew in on his exit, sending a shiver down her spine. She stepped near the stove to recover the heat. Glancing at the clock, the image of biscuits popped into her mind, and she opened the oven door. The light golden tops told her they were ready, and she withdrew the pan and placed it on the countertop. Her husband insisted fresh biscuits be made every day regardless if the previous day's batch

114

had been consumed. She didn't mind most days but at times, it forced her to eat more biscuits than she preferred. Hearing the creak of a door, she looked up to see her husband walk into the kitchen, as if by smell he knew the goods had left the oven.

"Would not be morning without this delight," Robert said as he hugged her. "And you make the best delights." He kissed her cheek and plucked a biscuit from the pan. "Hot, hot," he said, moving it from one hand to the other until he found a plate. "The butter will be milk again." He grinned and cut open the biscuit, releasing a cloud of steam. The butter he spread melted into the pours of the dough and disappeared, leaving only a light yellow behind.

Bessie chuckled. "You and your biscuits." Her joy did not come from baking them but from watching him eat them.

"The day I cannot start with biscuits would be a tragic day indeed." He snatched three more for his plate and retreated to the table.

She set to work preparing the eggs, porridge and tea. When Angus returned, she sent him to rouse his siblings. The busy day ahead did not allow any time for her family to dawdle. They needed to be off to work and school to give her time and space to do her chores. She glanced at the clock: 8:05. Two hours had passed since she rose from her warm bed, and she'd see another fourteen before she returned to it.

Hours later, with the sun low in the sky, she stirred the steaming pork soup in the large cauldron on the stove top. Her three youngest children had arrived home from school and were completing their lessons by the dying sunlight at the kitchen table. She'd soon light the oil lamp, but she'd wait until necessary to conserve the fuel. Robert's work in the coaling yard at the pier provided a good wage, but there was no room for waste.

She glanced at the wood box and frowned. Angus had yet to come home from school though she had given strict instructions for him to do so. His siblings said he had stayed behind to talk to one of the teachers for extra help, but she doubted this story. Angus was a bright student but not one to concern himself with his studies to spend more time than necessary in the classroom.

115

At sixteen, his interests dwelt more on the unhealthy relationship with a foreign woman.

"What is Angus doing at the Miller's?" asked Catherine.

Bessie shot her youngest, only eight, a questionable glare. *Indeed, what was he doing there?* She marched to the window and peeked out in time to see Angus follow the young *Fräulein* Greta into the Müller house. She spun, removed her house apron and tossed it on the back of a chair. Slipping on her woollen coat, boots and scarf, she went to the door.

"Behave yourselves, children." She looked at her second oldest, only fourteen. "Hattie, tend to your siblings and watch the soup." She swung open the door and stomped across the cobblestone street, avoiding pedestrians, horses and carts. When she reached the Müller door, she thwacked it several times. As she waited for an answer, she glanced about the street filled mostly with men returning home from work or running last minute errands. She heard the door open and turned to face Elisabeth Müller. A warm smell of boilt cabbage assaulted her senses. Elisabeth's hair was pulled up in a loose bun, leaving strands of greying hair dangling on either side of her round face. "I believe my son is here, Mrs. Müller."

Elisabeth's smile dimmed. "Yes, yes." She shouted over her shoulder in her terse heavily-accented voice. "Angus, your mamma has called for you." She returned her gaze to Bessie. "Vould you like to come in?"

Bessie watched her lips struggle with the English words. The woman had improved her language greatly since she moved to the area five years earlier. She told Bessie that before her family came to Canada, they had lived for three years in London, England. "Thank you." She forced a smile. "But I have no time for socializing. I need Angus home."

She nodded and let her gaze fall slightly.

Bessie lifted her head, looked over the German's shoulder and saw her son walk out of a backroom. His blank face turned to surprise, then worry. She tilted her head and narrowed her eyes to let him know she was displeased with his actions. She watched him mumble something out the side of his mouth to

116

Greta, gave her a quick glance and walked to the door.

"Mother," he said solemnly. He slipped on his jacket and boots and waited to pass between the two women. "I was only helping Greta with her lessons."

"I was told extra help was with your teacher." Bessie stepped away from the door opening to allow her son to exit the home.

"Yes, Ma'am." He held his hat in his hand as he stopped at the threshold and turned back. "Thank you, Mrs. Miller." He looked past her and nodded quickly at Greta, then entered into the twilight-lit Halifax street.

"Have a good evening, Mrs. Tucker," Elisabeth said.

"And the same to you." Bessie followed her son home in silence. When they reached the stoop, she spoke. "Angus, this girl is a bad influence."

He gave her a defiant look. "Mother, I—"

"You are responsible for filling the wood box, and this is twice in two days you failed to complete your chores."

"But, Mother, I am..."

Though the light was scarcely available, she watched his cheeks flush. "Son, your chores come first, and this *Fräulein*," she whispered, glancing over her shoulder to see if anyone listened, "is below you. Our brave Canadian soldiers are fighting her relatives on the front line."

"Mother," he snapped. "She's not like that. Greta and her family support the British. They are here because they feared for their lives in Germany."

"But they are still the enemy."

"Greta would never hurt me, and Mrs. Miller is a kind woman. They just want to be safe, Mother."

"And if the Germans attack Halifax?" She raised a sharp eyebrow. "Which side will they be on when German soldiers invade?"

Angus huffed. "It's getting late. Let me fill the wood box."

"Fine." She swung open the door and directed him inside. As she pulled off her outdoor clothes, she watched him scuttle out the back door to the woodpile. The boy had a lot to learn, and though she wanted him to stay young and avoid the call to duty to fight overseas, he needed to grow up and realise his responsibilities.

~ ⚭ ~

The next morning, Bessie struggled with the frozen water in the chicken coop, delaying her return to the wood stove. The fire was not burning hot enough, so she adjusted the damper to increase the flames. She placed the dipper of frozen water she had poured the evening before onto the stovetop to thaw to use for biscuits. As it melted, she prepared the other ingredients and put on a pot of tea. She glanced at the clock: 7:40. There was plenty of time to prepare the biscuits before Robert left for the pier. She tested his shirt, still hanging behind the stove to complete the drying. She felt no moisture within. For the next twenty minutes, she scurried around, mixing up the dough, cutting it into circles with a cup and slipping the biscuits into the warmed oven. Brushing a strand of hair from her cheek, she saw she was quickly running out of time.

"I smell them, but..." Robert waltzed into the kitchen and wrapped his arms around her. His strong arms held her tightly. "It seems my treats are sleeping late."

She giggled. "They will be out soon."

A knock came at the door.

"I think someone wishes to steal my biscuits." Robert released her and opened the door. A young man, no more than fifteen, in dark cloths stood straight, his hat in his hand.

"Mr. Tucker, sir." He adjusted his stance. "Mr. Patterson is requesting your immediate presence at the coaling yard. He has sent me to gather a crew."

"Slow down, Hans." Robert rubbed his chin. "What is the cause?"

"A ship needs to get underway immediately and needs to be fueled." The boy hesitated. "I am to give you his apologies for disturbing you before I rush off, sir, but I need to visit three more homes before returning to Pier 6."

"Of course." Robert nodded. "I'll see to it. Run along and get the other fellows."

Hans nodded and left the door.

Robert turned to Bessie. "The biscuits?" He smiled at her. "Will they be lunch?"

She rolled her eyes. "Only for you." She hugged and kissed him. "I'll deliver them myself." She watched him don his outer work clothes. When they had met more than eighteen years ago, she knew he was the one she'd love for the rest of her life. He knew what to say and do to sweep her off her feet, and it didn't matter what her mama said, she married him the day after he asked.

At the open door, he paused and beckoned her near. Kissing her once more, he held her tightly. "The cold may chill my cheeks, but you warm my heart."

"Such silliness." She giggled and released him reluctantly. "Off with you now. I'll see you in a few hours."

He gave her that smile he delivered when he laid her down in bed, tipped his hat and turned towards the street.

Bessie went to work, preparing breakfast for her four children. Her bones ached from the approaching storm. If she had time to place a warm cloth on her knees, she would, but time was not her friend today. It was 8:05. The children needed to rise if they were not to be late for school. She heard the rumble of the milk wagon stop across the street but did not look through the icy window. Instead, she hollered up the stairs for her children. One-by-one, they shuffled into the kitchen, rubbing sleep from their eyes. They were soon fed, dressed and preparing for the walk to school.

"Where is Angus?" Bessie watched her children pull on their outdoor clothes.

"He left right after eating," said Hattie. "Something about walking Greta to school."

Bessie grumbled inside but remained silent. She glanced at the clock: 8:58. School started at 9:15.

A rapid knock came at the door.

"Hurry, children," she said. "You don't want to be late." She opened the door and saw one of her neighbours standing there, flushed and anxious. "What's wrong, George?"

"The smoke," he stammered. "Fills the sky. A ship. Two ships. Fire. Boom!"

Bessie smiled. The man was simple and boasted about seeing many strange things. "Thank you, George."

He frantically glanced at her and each of her children, then towards the harbour. "It's on fire. Fire! Run for your lives!" He ripped his hat off his head and clung to it with white knuckles. "Mother is waiting. I run. Tell her. The fire." With that, he raced away from the door towards his house in the distance.

Bessie watched him go, shaking her head. He meant well and was harmless. Whatever fire he spoke of was far from here and probably a manifestation of his imagination. She was about to close the door when she saw a column of black smoke rising from the harbour. She paused and watched the dark mushroom top grow. It was unusually large for a simple fire.

"Momma, what's that?" Catherine stood by her side.

"I'm not sure," she said. "Perhaps I should see." She ushered her daughter inside. "Stay here, children. Don't leave until I return." She pulled her woollen jacket off the hook, pulled her scarf tight around her neck and stepped outside. Not far from her stoop was a street heading down to the waterfront. She walked to it, avoiding the morning bustle of the city. As she looked down the long hill, she watched crowds congregate near the waterfront, but she was too far away to make out who was there. The fire was a spectacle that attracted a lot of attention. She decided it was nothing for her to concern herself with and began for home.

In an instant, she felt her cheeks suck inward and she toppled to the ground with a heavy weight upon her. For long moments, she struggled to realise what had happened. The early morning sky grew dark and the usual rumble of carts and wagons was replaced with silence. Then a mass of commotion began, throbbing against her eardrums with such intensity, she thrust her hands against her ears. She cried out but failed to hear her voice. As she grappled with the noise, a severe pain shot up through her leg, almost dragging her into the depths of her

120

subconscious. She fought against it and forced her eyes to see the sights around her.

The scene made her gasp and she choked on dust. People and horses were rushing by, terror in their eyes. The street was littered with debris that continued to rain down upon it and pedestrians who, like her, had fallen to the ground. She attempted to push herself to her feet, but sharp objects dug into her skin.

"The Germans attacked!"

Bessie gawked at the young man who raced by, shouting like a maniac. His clothes were torn and blackened.

"Arm yourself! The Germans are coming!"

She watched him race out of sight, unable to move. Then she remembered her children. They were home alone. With a mighty shove, she propelled herself to a seated position. The pain in her hands throbbed and when she looked, she saw blood seeping around shards of glass embedded into her skin. That's when she noticed all the windows had blown out of the homes, leaving the insides open to the elements.

Her children. Home alone. She took a deep breath and tried to stand. Her left leg refused her orders, remaining twisted in an odd angle. Thoughts of her children injured swelled in her mind, sending a primitive howl from her lips.

"Mrs. Tucker."

She looked up to find her neighbour's son, Alexander, hovering over her. His eyes were wide with fear, his face dirtied from soot. "Help me stand."

The young man pulled on her arms and although smaller than she, managed to get her to her feet where she teetered.

"Please help me home," she begged.

Alexander nodded. Looking up at her, he asked in a quivering voice, "Did the Germans attack?"

She held her left thigh and pulled her leg forward. The pain brought red to her eyes and she clenched her teeth. "Dear, boy," she gasped. "I know not who has done this." She stumbled and spit flew from her mouth as the agony exploded. Through heavy breathing, she said, "A fire. Ships in the harbour." Tears fogged her eyes and in the shuffle of people and animals and the prattle filling her mind, she did not know where she was. Her body wanted to rest, to lie here on the cold hard ground and sleep. It beckoned her and if not for Alexander pulling her along, she would have done so.

"Mother!"

The scream pierced her ears and forced her eyes to clear. "Catherine." Behind her followed two of her other children, Hattie and James. They raced up to her and threw their arms around her. She tried to hold them, but the pain in her hands ached.

"Fire, Mother. Fire!" cried Catherine.

"I know, dear," Bessie said. "The ships in the harbour."

"No, Mother," said Hattie. "The house is on fire."

"What?" She stood taller and craned her neck to see the small house that lay about two hundred feet away. Smoke billowed out the windows. The house beside hers was also on fire. Her heart fell and she swallowed hard. She coughed on the smoke filling the air and the black dust that fell from the sky. Unable to hold her balance further, she collapsed to the ground, taking Alexander with her.

"Mother!" James and Hattie screamed together and reached down to help her up.

"Let me rest, children." Her breathing became ragged.

"What can we do?" Alexander asked.

"We need to get her inside," Hattie said, "before she freezes to death."

"But our house is on fire." James looked around. "Lorenz!"

Before Bessie could speak, he raced across the street to the Müller home. Elisabeth's son, the same age as Hattie, was huddled close to the door watching the chaos. She watched the two exchange words, then Lorenz pulled a wooden push wagon from beside the dwelling and rushed over with James by his side.

"Mrs. Tucker, your leg." Lorenz ogled her limp appendage. His

English was perfect.

"I'll be fine," she said.

"Mother." James frowned at her. He directed Lorenz to turn the wagon. "Help me get her inside."

"This is not necessary," mumbled Bessie.

"Quiet, Mother," Hattie said, holding her arm. "We learnt emergency procedures in school. Alexander, help me on this side. James and Lorenz, hold her on that side. Catherine, steady the wagon."

Pain gripped Bessie as they moved her from the ground to the wooden wagon. She cried out when her leg twisted, but James quickly supported it, nulling the throbbing. Once in the wagon, James and Lorenz pushed it slowly across the street.

A large man scuttled by mumbling to himself in strange words. He was covered in blood and soot. She could not determine the colour of his skin nor the language he spoke. His face was damaged beyond recognition, with pieces of skin dangling from his cheeks. He stumbled, fell, only to rise again and continue his journey into the sea of smoke and wandering souls.

When they reached the Müller home, Lorenz ran inside, leaving the door open. Elisabeth rushed out. When she saw Bessie, her hands flew to her mouth.

"*Furchtbar!*" For a moment, she was frozen in place. Her gaze flew over the shadows scampering in the street.

"Mama." Lorenz pulled on her arm. "She needs help."

Elisabeth hopped into action. "Veel her closer. Vee must carry her inside." She motioned them closer to the door. She put up her hand to stop them when they reached the threshold. "Easy. Boys, hold her sides." She put her hands under Bessie's arms and prepared to lift her. "Zis vill hurt."

Bessie watched the cold blue eyes sweep over her face as she warned her about the pain. Why was this woman helping her if Germans were invading the city?

"Lorenz, Alexander, lift." Elisabeth steadied her as the boys hoisted her from the wagon. Then she guided her to the daybed next to the stove.

Bessie tried to slow her descent by grasping the bed. Clamping her teeth together, she braced herself against the pain. She reluctantly released a whimper as she rested her back against the cushion and Elisabeth eased her injured leg onto the bed. The pain raced through her body as quickly as runaway horses galloped through the city.

"Children, come inside. Sit. Sit." Elisabeth ushered Bessie's children to the kitchen table.

"I must get home to Mother," Alexander said. "She may need my help."

"Alex, if you cannot find your family, come here," Elisabeth said. "You vill be safe here."

He nodded, then raced from the doorway.

Elisabeth closed the door, sealing much of the chaos outside. She rushed about, gathering water, rags and other material, then sat next to Bessie. "I vould call for doctor, but they vould be busy, and these vounds must be treated." She turned to her daughter, no more than twelve. "Get me the blanket from the bed."

The blonde girl raced off and returned within seconds, holding a heavy blanket tightly in her arms.

Elisabeth spread it over Bessie, leaving only her arms, head and left leg exposed. She set the oil lantern closer to the daybed, placed a smaller, folded blanket beneath the leg and examined the injury. "It is broken," she said. "And has glass in it." She looked up and forced a smile. "I vill do my best."

Bessie gripped the German's arm. "You are not a doctor."

Elisabeth shook her head. "But as a young voman I helped tend to men injured by farming or in battles. My mother showed me the vay."

She swallowed hard, fearing the German would remove her leg or inflict more damage. Glancing at her three children huddled around the small wooden table with Lorentz, staring at her as if the world was about to end, a lump formed in her throat. If she didn't let the woman perform crude surgery on her leg, she might bleed to death and leave them motherless.

124

A loud thud erupted above the sounds of carts and screaming people, shaking her to her core. Through the glassless window, she saw the panicked crowd and the opposite side of the street where fire tore through her home. Yet this side of the street, though battered, stood strong.

"Bessie, it must be done." Elisabeth came close to her face. "Vat happens out there will only vorsen in here if the bleeding is not stopped."

She melted into the daybed, surrendering to the pain and the circumstances dealt her. Nodding, she whispered, "Please, see to my children."

"Of course." Elisabeth gave her a wooden spoon. "If the pain is unbearable, bite down on this."

She held the spoon in her shaky, blood-covered hand. As she felt Elisabeth run cool water over her injured leg, she placed the wood between her teeth and held it firm. Closing her eyes and sending her thoughts on a wild trip across the Citadel and into the forest, she attempted to ignore what was to come. The agony slowly grew with each touch, tug and wipe, and she moaned uncontrollably. Shock waves travelled up her spine and exploded in her head, and she recoiled. The pain became too much and she slipped into unconsciousness.

~ ❦ ~

The sound of wood snapping and cracking stirred Bessie from a deep slumber. As thoughts blossomed slowly and linked together to form memories, her heart raced. Her house was on fire. She forced open her eyes and tried to sit up but failed to gather the strength.

"Mother." Hattie sat beside her on the daybed and stared into her face. "You're alive." A tear slipped down the young girl's cheek. "Oh, Mother." She rested her head upon her bosom and sobbed.

"Dear, child, of course I'm alive." Bessie patted her head and held her trembling body with bandaged hands.

"So many people did not survive."

"The fire in the harbour," Bessie said. "Our home." When her daughter looked up, she noticed swelling around her reddened

125

eyes as if she had spent much time crying. "I will be fine. Do not worry yourself. You mustn't cry."

"But I must. I cry for Angus and Greta and everyone who is dead. And the dying; oh, the sounds of the dying."

The wind left Bessie's lungs and she gulped to recapture it. Her eldest had left for school early and had not returned. "Where is Angus?"

Hattie sobbed harder. "Mr. Colps said he saw him and Greta running towards the harbour to see the fire. He said they wouldn't have survived the blast that close to the water." She threw herself into her mother's arms.

She clutched her child, unable to believe the words she spoke. If no one near the harbour survived, then...Robert...Pier 6. Her husband and her son had been...She crushed the thought. She would not believe it. It was a lie. A great flood of heat moved through her limbs and congregated around her heart, hindering her breathing. She gulped for air and felt the sting of tears on her cheeks. *Her Robert was safe. She would deliver biscuits to him for lunch. Angus was safe. He was dawdling near the wood pile.* The image of her husband and son smiling at her froze in her mind. They were well and would be home soon. But she wasn't there. They could be looking for her at this moment.

"Bessie, you should eat."

When she looked up, she found Elisabeth hovering over her.

"It vill help you regain your strength. I vill fix you something." Elisabeth picked up a bowl and went to the stove where a large pot rested.

"Where is Angus?" Bessie asked.

Elisabeth's back straightened, and she stared into the distance. "He and Greta have not returned." Her voice, even in tone, discouraged further questioning. "This soup will keep you warm." She carried the bowl to the small table beside the daybed.

"If not for Greta, Angus would have been home with me." Her terse voice surprised her.

"And if not for Angus, Greta would be by my side." Elisabeth walked away and busied herself with cleaning dishes.

Bessie fell silent, her eyes darting around the dimly lit room, taking in the site of her young children, Elisabeth's children, the food and the meagre decorations. While she had slept, someone had placed blankets over the broken windows in an attempt to keep out the cold air, leaving the only light source the oil lamp.

"Mother," whispered Hattie close to her ear, "Mrs. Miller loves Greta as much as we love Angus." Her sad eyes pleaded with her. "And Mr. Miller has not returned." More tears slipped from her eyes. "Neither has Father."

Bessie gulped. Surely, they would return before day's end.

"You should eat, Mother." Hattie moved the bowl closer. "We must take care of ourselves and stick together. Father would not want us to cower fearfully." She forced a weak smile. "Mrs. Miller has offered us a place to stay until Father returns, so at least we won't freeze to death."

She nodded, wondering how her daughter had grown wise so quickly. Gripping the spoon, she scooped the thin soup into her mouth. The taste struck her tongue. While sharp, the flavour enticed her to eat more. By the time the bowl was emptied, she was sitting up straighter and more aware of her surroundings. Hattie had no sooner taken the bowl from her grasp when a heavy knock came to the door.

Elisabeth released a sharp gasp and rushed to open it.

The young man standing on the stoop wore clothes dirtied and torn from hard labour.

"You bring news?" Elisabeth waited, mouth open, as if she were about to hear the water had drained from the oceans.

"I've been sent for Mrs. Tucker. I was told I might find her here."

Bessie craned her neck to identify the man. The scene behind her, however, caught her attention. Smoke still meandered out of the row of houses across the street. The late afternoon sun, darkened by clouds, cast an eerie hue over the scene. The chaos on the street had slowed, with the occasional person, horse or cart ambling by. Gone was the frantic rush she had left behind when she entered the Müller household.

The man stepped closer, blocking her view, and she saw it was the same boy who had beckoned Robert away from the house earlier in the day. "Hans?"

"Yes, Ma'am." He pulled the hat from his head and stared at the floor. "The officer who gave me the grave news to deliver sends his regrets that he could not deliver it personally, but he hopes you will understand the extreme circumstances in which he is working."

"What news?" Bessie gripped the blankets tightly.

"Your husband, Mr. Tucker, was killed this morning during the explosion. He was one of seven men—"

A guttural wail escaped Bessie as she flung herself against the pillow. She had just kissed him goodbye, promised she'd deliver his biscuits for lunch. He couldn't be gone.

"Thank you," Elisabeth said to Hans. "It is better to know than to be left wondering." She ushered him towards the door. "I vill see to her."

Hans nodded and left without hesitation.

The next several hours delivered many more visitors to the door. They were neighbours who enquired about the family's condition or the whereabouts of members of their own family. Others were work associates of Elisabeth's husband who queried about his whereabouts. The shoe shop where he worked was not located in the hardest hit area of the city but close enough it had sustained damage. When the associates passed the shop, they noticed windows and doors had been ripped out, but the stone building stood while wooden structures around it had collapsed. No one gave news about the children though each was asked if they had seen Angus and Greta.

As the day gave way to evening, the women and children fell silent and kept busy with chores, reading or resting. Elisabeth reinforced the blankets over the windows as the temperature outside dropped. She had no sooner walked away from a window, when a loud thud hit the door. She flung it open, her facial expression hoping it to be someone she knew.

Bessie watched the expression fall. She knew she was looking for Greta and her husband Carl to arrive but with each visitor, Elisabeth slipped into a more solemn mood. Her words were fewer and her steps slower. This sudden bang propelled her to the door, perhaps because she suspected her loved ones were injured and had hit the door abruptly.

However, Carl, nor Greta or Angus stood on the stoop when the door opened this time. No one stood there except for a large stone.

"Germans!" a male voice shouted. "You did this to us! We'll get you!" The voice faded in the distance.

Elisabeth slammed the door shut. When she turned, her eyes were large and her face taut. "Ve did nothing!" she cried. "Ve are innocent." Her hands covered her face and she ran to a chair to sit.

Bessie watched, unable to move and unable to fathom why a stranger would do this to a woman and her children.

When a knock came at the door again, Bessie spoke up. "James, answer it."

Her twelve-year-old son hesitated.

"You and Hattie together."

Hattie and James opened the door. A policeman stood there with another officer behind him.

"Excuse me, but does Elizabeth live here?" asked the officer.

"I am Elizabeth," said Bessie.

The officer peeked into the house. "Elisabeth Müller?"

"I am Elizabeth Tucker," she said. "This is Elisabeth Miller. There is no Müller here."

Bessie glanced at Elisabeth who lifted her head and stared at her. Certainly, she knew Bessie was a nickname for Elizabeth.

"We are looking for Germans," said the officer. "We are to gather those who survived and retain them until we learn more about what caused the accident."

"Ridiculous," Bessie said. "This woman is a good friend of mine. I have known her for years. She is not German; she came here from London." She glanced around, hoping to provide proof. Seeing Elisabeth's son who spoke perfect English, she ushered him forward. "Lorenz, speak to the officer. Tell him your mother grieves because your father has not returned and is feared dead."

The boy's face fell and tears glistened in his eyes. "Father has not returned. His shoe shop was near the harbour. We pray he will be found alive. He is not a German spy, only a hardworking, honest shoemaker."

The officer nodded. "If you hear of any Germans in the area, please let us know." He tipped his hat and left the doorway.

Hattie closed the door shut, and Lorenz locked it.

Bessie gripped her hands, the bandages feeling awkward in her grip. As her eyes met Elisabeth's, her heart went out to her. The coming days might uncover their deception but tonight, the families—both the Tucker and Miller—would grieve their losses together.

∾

Liana Olive Quinn

Liana Olive Quinn lives in Nova Scotia, but she's flung her fedora in many interesting locales over the decades. She's delved into twisted and forbidden caves where hordes of bats watched her pass. She's strolled ancient tunnels carved into a harbour bank centuries beforehand to hide the questionable of minds. She's walked the dark streets of a mysterious village, wondering all the while if someone or something would pounce from the shadows. And then there are the cemeteries: beautiful by day, haunting by night.

Liana enjoys sharing her passion for the dark, the mysterious, the unimaginable through short stories. She is the author of *Gardening for Her Life*. For more information, visit her website https://lianaquinn.wordpress.com.

Big Ramblin' Mike

Annemarie Hartnett

MY FATHER WAS A GOOD MAN. This was what I told people after that long day. This was what I told his grandchildren, great-grandchildren and great great-grandchildren. I said it at his funeral in '52 and in every memorial I put into the paper on the anniversary of his death. When someone came collecting stories about the explosion and asked me about what Big Ramblin' Mike did, I told her and she put it in a book. Not everyone believed it, but that's fine. I know it's true.

Paw was the sort of man who'd shrug and say he only did what's right. That's what he was doing that morning when everything went to Hell. He ran a little shop that sold and repaired stoves and ovens, but he would also fix anything anyone brought him if he knew how to do it.

Mum got up with him that day, made his breakfast and ironed his shirt and slacks while he ate. She would have been waiting for him with supper ready when he came home. She called it habit after all these years, but I think she was just glad to have him at her kitchen table instead of wet and shivering in a trench in Belgium or France. She wanted to enjoy every meal with him she could because she said others weren't so lucky.

Paw said at his age, he'd be no good for service, but the real reason he couldn't fight was because he was almost blind in one eye. In his day, Paw could have taken out a whole mess of Huns with his fists alone. He had been a boxer and he'd taken a fist right to the eye one night, which ended his career.

As you'd expect of a boxer, Paw was a big man. He had massive shoulders, thick forearms, a barrel chest and legs like telephone poles. Mum used to say he was fierce looking. That was her way of saying how handsome she thought he was. He was from good Irish stock with thick black hair and brows. His skin was so dusky some folks asked if he was part Indian. We all took after him, all except for baby Nancy, who had inherited Mum's red-brown hair and pale skin.

And Mum—oh, he was *on fire* for her. That's how he always put it, especially when he got into the liquor. "The first time I saw her on the ferry with her mother, I was *on fire* for her," he'd slur whenever one of the grandchildren asked him about her.

It was a wonder he could carry on after he lost her that day. There were nights for years afterward, I heard him in his bed, choked by rasping sobs that came from the bottom of his gut, but he never faltered. Not once. Not after he lost her and not on that day. He kept going because that's what he did, and what he had to do to keep himself from going mad with his grief.

Just as Paw was where he should have been when it happened, so was I–on my way to school with Benjy shrieking at me to *wait up* in that babyish whine of his.

At the exact moment it happened, I'd heard enough of him. I was eleven and I was impatient to be rid of him and off to play with boys my own age. I spun around to face him but before I could say anything, I saw what I thought was the sun light up his face and cast my shadow long and ominous in front of me.

It hurt. It hurt badly. There was so much heat coming at me at once. Instinct made me plant my feet on the sidewalk, but there was nothing beneath my soles. I couldn't see. One minute it felt as though my eyes were being blown into my skull and in the next as if they were being sucked from the sockets. One breath and my throat closed against the brimstone that filled my lungs.

I sprawled where I had landed, clenching and unclenching my fists and blinking hard through the sting in my eyes. I couldn't hear a thing, the ringing in my ears was so shrill.

Finally, I heard voices in shouts, cries and shrieks. I pushed up and rubbed my eyes, but that only made the pain worse. There was something grimy on my hands I couldn't rub away, so I yanked open my jacket and rubbed my face with the clean shirt underneath.

It took another moment before the blur faded, and I discovered I was in someone's parlour. The furniture had been thrown to one end of the room along with me. Grasping the leg of the overturned sofa, I pulled myself to my feet and stood there a moment longer, gaping at the hole in the front of the room. This house, whomever it belonged to, had a bite taken out of it. Through the haze in the air, I saw the road covered in debris.

I saw Benjy, half-reclined on the opposite side of the street, his face smeared with blood. He was screaming for Mum. When he saw me emerge from the house, his eyes grew wide, and he held his arms out as he used to do to Mum when he was small. He shrieked my name in one long moan. "*Haaaaaaank-eeeeeee!*"

I didn't say anything as I pulled him to his feet, nor when he shrieked louder and I picked him up. Arms and legs wrapped tight around me, he kept on blubbering.

"We have to get out of here," I murmured to no one in particular but as I looked around, I felt hopeless. We lived on Russell Street, but I could see few streets around us. If it wasn't for the harbour below, I would have thought we had been picked up and carried to a nightmarish wasteland. There were houses torn in two and some gone completely. My view of the harbour was unobstructed compared to moments ago when I could only glimpse the water down the streets when I crossed them. The water now moved as it did during storms, and it had an oily film on it. Broken ships bobbed on its surface. I could see people struggling to make it to the shore.

Above the water was a black cloud, swollen as if it had belched out this carnage and was inhaling to let out another.

"I want Mummy!" Benjy cried against my neck, leaving a slime of snot and spit against my collar.

Hugging him closer, I muttered, "Me, too," and walked into

that hellish landscape.

I zigzagged this way and that, trying to get some sense of direction. I stopped and squeezed my eyes shut to conjure the memory of my school route in my head. I'd done it hundreds of times, and I should have been able to come up with something, a landmark to look for, something I could remember as a beacon to tell me I was close to home, but there was nothing there. Things I should have known had been pushed out and replaced with things I should have never seen—the bloodied, the burnt, the torn apart. I considered sitting down and waiting for someone to tell me what to do when Benjy was suddenly snatched from me. I came back to life instantly, ready to fight to keep him.

My father stood before me with Benjy shaking in his beefy arms. Before I could cry out, Paw had me off my feet and was madly kissing the both of us on our dirty cheeks.

I can't remember what he said or what I said. I just remember the hot tears running down my face, the oily smell around us and Paw's arm squeezing me so tightly I couldn't breathe. We were all speaking at once in incoherent words of relief and panic.

"We have to go," he said at last, pulling away from me as he looked towards the direction of home. "Someone said the magazine is on fire. We have to get to cover."

"What about Mum and the babies?"

"We'll find them."

I remember the conviction in his voice. We'd find the others. He'd find his Mary Jane and his little Ellen, Nicholas, Maud and Nancy.

I had a million questions for him as we joined the exodus of people quickly moving south, but I didn't ask any of them. I was sure he'd know the answer to everything, but all three of us lapsed into silence as we walked.

We waited on Citadel Hill for two hours with hundreds of other people. Paw spit into his handkerchief and cleaned our faces, then looked for cuts. I had dozens, though none serious. Benjy had a nasty gash at his hairline and a broken ankle. When the all clear came, Paw carried him and clutched my hand as we headed for home. He knew right where to find it, knew exactly which house was ours, though we discovered there wasn't much house left to find.

"Stay here," Paw told us, and I sat with Benjy on my lap as he started digging.

"This isn't home," Benjy whimpered.

I wanted to agree with him, but something—maybe that same instinct that told Paw where to look—told me this was our home, had been our house.

A few others joined him as he dragged away the debris of our house. When he found Maud, Paw collapsed onto one knee and wept into his hand as they pulled her out. A soldier who had been helping with the rescue marched up to us and went about wrapping Benjy's ankle. He blocked my line of sight as Nicholas was laid out on the grass next to Maud.

I didn't recognise Nancy. She was so little and limp in his arms, I thought they had pulled out one of Maud's baby-dolls.

Then came a cry of "Paw-Paw!" and out came two-year-old Ellen, wide-eyed and white with plaster. She almost turned purple in his desperate embrace and wailed to be let loose.

I couldn't look when Mum was carried out. I dropped my head on Ellen's chalky shoulder and squeezed my eyes shut.

It was dark when we finally left. Paw didn't say anything to Benjy about the others or Mum, but he held me closer and let me cry into his filthy shirt. We had nowhere to go so went to Paw's store.

The only light came from kerosene lanterns and the stove in the rear of the store. Once Paw nailed oilcloth over the broken windows, the shop front became toasty warm.

He stripped us down and inspected for more serious injuries but aside from the cuts and Benjy's busted ankle, there were none. Not even Ellen, who had the house come down around her, had more than a dirty cut on her shoulder—though she did complain of terrible headaches the rest of her life and blamed the explosion.

Wrapping the three of us in a dirty tarp, Paw gave us an exhausted smile with a bit of pork roast from his uneaten lunch.

He pushed his big hand through my hair, then hissed and jerked back. There was fresh blood on his fingers.

"There's glass in your hair, Hanky," he murmured, then quickly rooted out a pair of shears.

For the next hour, he hummed *Whiskey in The Jar* as he snipped my hair nearly to the roots and plucked what glass he could find from my scalp. He did the same to Benjy and Ellen, muttering how Mum would be devastated Ellen's lovely black curls were gone.

At the mention of Mum, Benjy whimpered. "When is Mummy coming?"

"Tomorrow," Paw said, throwing me a look. I hadn't known then why it had to be a secret between the two of us, but I know now he was too exhausted to tell his remaining children their mother was never coming. They were little, we were tired and it could wait.

As he carried a fussy Ellen across the creaking floor and spoke soothing words to lull her to sleep, a rattle came at the door. Paw froze, and Benjy and I huddled closer together.

"Lie down and cover your heads," Paw whispered as he passed Ellen to us. "Don't make a sound until I tell you to."

We did what we were told, but I made sure there was a sliver in the blanket for me to look out of.

Paw opened the door a crack. Words were shared, then Paw stepped aside. Two women came in, followed by a soldier in soot-stained khaki.

"How many more can you take?" the soldier asked my father, who looked around and pushed his fingers through his hair with a shrug.

"As many as I can, I suppose," he said and after the soldier left, he turned to the women. "What're your names?"

"Marianne and Lucille," said the one who had her arm around the other.

"My name is Mike, and these are my children."

We pulled off our cover and gawped at the women, both in

their nightgowns underneath the massive pea coat they shared.

Paw teased me many years later about them being prostitutes from Montreal, come to Halifax to take advantage of the glut of activity in the city. "Christ, it's a wonder my Mary Jane didn't come back to life to give me hell for spending the night with a couple of short-time girls."

Then came the Denny family, or what was left of them; two girls my age and their grandmother; Evangeline Hodder, a factory girl from Newfoundland; and Robert and Agnes Bell, and their infant daughter Katherine. A whole mess of people came in at once from a cart directed by the soldier who had appeared earlier at the door. Paw nearly fell over himself getting folks situated and comfortable in both the front and back rooms. The soldier brought a crate of supplies, then shook Paw's hand and disappeared into the night.

The sudden activity was both exciting and terrifying. Ellen stopped crying and looked around, tugging my coat to ask, "Hanky, who that?" about everyone. Benjy openly commented on the injuries that came through the door, but no one scolded him as being impolite.

Everyone told their stories of survival, where they had been when *it* happened and who amongst their people had died or were missing.

Then came the arguing about what *it* was. Germans, most agreed, but a few insisted it had been two ships in the harbour running into one another. *Saw it with my own eyes*, they said.

Voices lowered as folks nodded off. Benjy was amongst the first to go, while Ellen refused to lay her head down until she was in Paw's arms, after which she was passed back to me.

I couldn't sleep. My head was too filled with everything— the suffocating smell of everyone around me, the oil on their clothes, the coppery scent of their blood, their body odour, the voices and the stories they told, and the remembrance of what the day had brought.

I missed my mother, my brother and sisters. Though I knew they were dead, I couldn't shake the feeling they were cold, that Nicholas waited on Paw to tell him about the fights he'd won, that Maud wanted a song or that Nancy gurgled in her crib, that Mum was anxious for us to return, so she could put on a pot of tea for Paw to drink while he beat me at cards before my bedtime.

It was through my blur of tears I first spotted Christophe.

I hadn't seen him enter the shop, and I didn't remember hearing his story. He sat in the shadowy corner facing the rest of the room. He was blonde and fair, even with the soot smeared on him, with pale eyes behind broken spectacles. Long, lanky legs folded close to him. He clutched a suitcase against his chest.

Paw, who made sure everyone had something to cover themselves, had turned his attention back to us and followed my gaze.

The man's eyes grew wide as Paw approached. I thought to myself that he must not have ever seen a man as big and strong as Paw.

"Did you get a cup of tea, fella?" Paw asked, his tone as gentle as when he spoke to everyone else in the room.

The man quickly averted his gaze, then gave his head a mad little shake.

Paw squatted, his posture as if he was trying to coax a stray pup to his hand.

"You should at least have something to eat. Some porridge or bread with molasses would do you good."

Lids still lowered and pale blonde lashes fluttering, the man simply shook his head. He reminded me of a spider backed into a corner, making itself so small it was as though it hoped to appear as nothing more than a speck amidst the dust.

Paw had given each person a gentle touch after he had attended to them: a squeeze on the shoulder, a hand held inside his big mitt or greasy hair pushed away from tired eyes. Not with this man. Paw didn't lay a finger on him or persist. He lingered a moment longer before getting to his feet.

"Is he hurt?" I whispered when Paw took a seat with us.

The floorboards creaked as he shifted to get comfortable,

then draped his arm around my shoulders.

"Maybe," he murmured. "Maybe not. He could be stunned by what happened, like when you banged your noggin on the bannister that time and you couldn't see or think straight for three days."

I smiled, and then the memory of the house that wasn't there any longer made my throat close up, and I pressed my face into his chest. Paw stank, but it didn't matter to me. He was warm and he made me feel safe.

"Where will we live?" I managed when my sobbing stopped.

"We'll figure something out, Hanky."

The thing you have to remember is these were good people, but they were scared. Everyone was scared. Even after they found out it was an accident, many persisted in believing the Germans had done it. We were at war, and the threat wasn't paranoia: U-boats were spotted along the coast, and spies had been captures. Good people sometimes did bad things when they were scared unless there's someone to stop them. That's what Paw told me.

Though, maybe they were just bad people. I don't know. I truly don't know.

I suppose Christophe was lucky he had chosen Paw's store for shelter. Part of me wanted to think that no matter where the frightened young man ended up, someone would have stood up for him.

It was still dark when it happened. I had managed to fall into a sleep so deep that when I was wrenched out of it, I remained foggy and confused about the shapes around me. I heard someone cry, "No! No, please! Leave me be!" and then I heard Paw growl out a curse.

Ellen was already awake and whimpering in my lap, while Benjy had wormed behind me and clung to my back as a baby animal ready to be carried across rushing water.

Paw was on his feet in front of Christophe, facing away from the wide-eyed man. He held a coal shovel like a knight might brandish a sword, but it wasn't his weapon that made him frightful. It was his stance. The big man seemed twice his size,

139

and his expression challenged the three men and one woman who stood before him.

Christophe had been talking in his sleep. Others had listened, and they didn't like what they heard.

"You know we're right, Mike," the woman said in a hiss. "What they did to us—they're all guilty."

Paw gave a shake of his head. "I told you twice already, if you want to make trouble, you can get out of my store. You can go out there and freeze to death."

"For Christ's sake, get out of the way, so I can bash his filthy skull in." One of the men snarled and dared a step forward.

Paw lifted the shovel slightly, and it was enough to stop the man. Paw's nostrils flared, his upper lip curled and his eyes glittered in the dim lamplight.

"Sit back down. All of you," he said through his bared teeth.

"No one will know," the woman replied. "There are so many bodies out there, one more won't be—"

"Listen to yourself!" This came from a woman seated on the bench by the front window. "Mike is right. You're being foolish and cruel. We don't need this tonight."

"No one will know," the other woman persisted.

A sound like I'd never heard before came out of my father, low and rumbling, and the muscles in his massive shoulders bunched.

"I'll know. My children will know. Everyone in this room will know." He held out his arm towards the young man cowering in his shadowy corner. "You think he had something to do with this? If it were the Germans and he had something to do with it, you think he has nowhere better to go than here? That he wouldn't have been out of town as soon as it happened?"

The aggressors faltered. The woman's mouth opened and closed without a word passing over her tongue. The men exchanged glanced. All stood firm.

"What's in the bag then?" the woman asked.

"What's in yours?" Paw snapped back.

"Now, you look here—"

"No, *you* look here. You're not putting a finger on this fella unless you want to go through me first. There may be more of you but so help me, I'll lay each one of you flat and then I'll put you out in the cold."

The men took a step forward, and the young woman who spoke before did so again. "Maybe, Mike, you could ask the young man to show us what's in the bag. So everyone can see it's harmless."

It was Paw's turn to falter.

That might have been the easiest way to settle things, he conceded years later, but he didn't trust the easy way. Christophe might have opened his bag and something harmless might have been construed as dangerous.

Or Paw could have been wrong, and the man hiding in the corner could have been the spy and saboteur they thought he was, and he'd have something to blow us to smithereens.

"What he's got in his bag is none of my business and none of yours. If you want him to show what he's got, then every one of us has to do the same—and don't think I didn't hear some of you whispering about how you'd been looting before you came here."

It was a good bluff. As he later said, these were good people, but they were scared. That made them opportunistic.

"This is how it's going to be," Paw went on. "If anyone so much as looks at this fella funny, I'll bury this here shovel in their throat. We're all here together because we're cold and we have nowhere else to go. We're going to take care of one another. If anyone has an issue with that, they can find out how they fare in the blizzard out there."

He tossed the shovel aside and crossed his arms over his broad chest, and he looked not just to those who stood before him but everyone, even us children. It was a challenge for everyone. *Try me*, his whole body seethed.

No one questioned him. He drew a deep, swelling breath and swung around enough to glance at the young man behind him.

"If we've had enough of this nonsense for one night, I suggest everyone try and get some sleep. Are we clear?" They nodded, and he gestured to his children. "Over here, Hanky."

Dragging my sister and half-carrying my brother with me, I scooted to his side and we resettled. We made a small barrier in front of the man who was still gaping with terror.

"You got a name, fella?" Paw asked after a few moments. His legs stretched out in front of him. Ellen was asleep on his lap, and Benjy and I were tucked beneath his arms.

The man hesitated, watching Paw closely, then pulled off his broken glasses and rubbed his eyes. "Christophe Huber."

"Michael Roache, and here is Henry, Benjamin and Ellen. How long have you been in Halifax?"

"March. I lived in North Carolina since I was his age." He gestured to me, then quickly looked away when our gazes met.

I suppose it had something to do with my startled expression at his accent. Hun! Enemy! I pictured a propaganda poster I had seen at a recruiting station where a German soldier leered back at me with devilish eyes that promised nightmares.

"I came here on my way to Cape Breton where my sister lives. She's married to a Canadian man from Port Hood."

With a deep sigh, he set his bag alongside him. All eyes were upon him, and everyone held their breath as he opened the bag and reached inside.

He pulled out a book that at first glance I could tell was a Bible. It was huge with a leather cover and gilt-edged pages. The spine creaked as he opened it. He flipped to the back where there were scribbles over two pages, and he pointed to one of those scribbles.

"Nadja Scott, my sister; her husband, Albert; and her three children, Catherine, Patrick and Ada," he said, running a dirty nail over the tree that had been drawn. "My mother and father are both dead, and my grandfather died last month. I have nowhere else to go, so I will work on their farm."

"Beautiful country up there."

He shook his head at the names in his book. "I do not think I will be good at farming. I taught school, but I could not do that any longer with the way people are."

Paw made a disgusted sound, and I received another shock when my father said something in the man's tongue.

Christophe gawped along with me, and Paw chuckled. "I was a boxer before I married. I fought a fellow by the name of Engel from Stuttgart, and I picked up a little from him as we travelled together."

"You should keep that to yourself. It is not good to speak German these days, as you have learned," Christophe said as he tucked his book into his bag. He settled, more or less, mirroring Paw's position with his legs stretched in front of him and his back to the wall, but the tension remained in his limbs.

"That's why you didn't say anything, isn't it?" Paw probed quietly. "Because everyone would know."

"This is a dangerous place for me right now," he said, glancing at the four aggressors glaring at us from the other side of the room.

They frightened me more than Christophe ever could. Such hatred directed not only at him but also at Paw, and I squeezed deeper into his embrace.

"I am surprised I made it here alive," Christophe went on. "When I saw you beckoning to me from the door, I almost did not come in, but I was so cold and so tired. I swore I would sit down and say nothing, and I would be the first to leave in the morning. I do not know if I will be able to leave this city without being arrested."

"I'll go with you," someone said.

We looked up to find the young woman who had earlier leapt to his defense standing over us. She held out her cup of tea to Christophe. Though hesitant, he took it nonetheless, and the woman settled in our little clique.

"I've got nowhere to go, and Cape Breton sounds as good as anywhere else. I can do the talking and tell anyone who asks that you're my husband and you lost your voice from the smoke."

She pulled her legs up underneath her, and I caught a glimpse of men's trousers and rubber boots under her dirty skirt. Annie, her name was, though we wouldn't find out until they both reached Port Hood and she wrote to us.

"Who did you lose?" Paw asked her.

"Everyone. My sisters and my father, and the aunt who was living with us. My sisters worked in the textiles factory with my father. I was at home taking care of Aunt Clara. They all died and I couldn't get Aunt Clara out, so here I am."

"My children lost their mother, along with their brother and sisters," he murmured.

I found it odd he didn't say 'my wife and children'. I asked him about it years later, and he said it was because it would be many weeks later before he could admit to himself that they were truly gone.

At that moment, he said his losses in a flat, sober tone that matched Annie's. She nodded, then turned back to Christophe.

"Well, what do you say? I'll help you and you'll help me? Give me a place to stay with your sister until I can find somewhere else. I know it's improper for an unmarried woman to travel with an unmarried man she just met and asking for a place to stay on top of that, but...it's not like either of us have much of a choice."

"I—" Christophe bit his lip, suspicion back in his troubled expression. He narrowed his eyes at Annie, studying her in silence, then nodded. "There will be room for you where I go. It is as Michael says. We must take care of one another." He looked to Paw. "You and your children, do you have a place to go?"

Paw smiled and looked around the room. "Right here, for now."

"You can come with us. My brother-in-law would be happy to have a man as big as you are to help him."

Paw's laugh vibrated through me. "I'd be worse at farming than you think you'll be. No, I have things to do here. We're better off than most. We can stay here if we have to."

No one spoke for the longest time, not until Christophe once again reached into his suitcase and pulled out something new. It was a flask, which he unscrewed and handed to Paw.

"For your hospitality."

Paw took it and sniffed the rim, then chuckled. "To your

health, Christophe."

He drank and passed the flask back. Christophe raised it and smiled. "And to your health and your children's health."

Without any words save for the occasional thanks, the bottle was passed throughout the shop. No one refused, not even the group who had wanted to kill Christophe for the sin of being German. Even I was given a small sip that made me sputter. Soon, most of us finally slept.

Paw kept watch all night.

Christophe and Annie left together in the morning to take the train to Port Hood. They remained friends their whole lives. Annie married a fellow from Mabou and Christophe moved west and started his own family. They wrote to Paw often, and Annie took the train for Paw's funeral in '52.

As for us, we stayed in the shop. Paw got beds and other things from the Relief Commission and made up a little space for us in the storeroom. We stayed there right up until our house was rebuilt. It was lean for a while. There wasn't much call for his wares in the early days but once insurance money started coming in and people started to rebuild, he found himself a busy man. He almost sent us to Kentville to live a while with family, but none of us could bear to be parted.

We buried Mum and the little ones in Mount Olivet cemetery. Paw never remarried. He spent his last days in a little bungalow in Spryfield where he could be found sitting on the porch with his radio even in cold weather.

I'm the only one left now who can remember that night. Benjy—Ben, as he likes to be called now—says he only remembers being thrown and breaking his ankle. He's walked with a limp his whole life. Ellen swears she remembers the house coming down on her, though only she knows if that's true. She was so little, I wouldn't expect her to remember anything, but the mind is a funny thing.

While he was alive, Big Ramblin' Mike was the name of a fighter folks vaguely remembered but after he died, the subsequent generations took an interest in what had happened that December morning. Big Ramblin' Mike became one of the disaster's mascots, the former boxer who gave shelter to those who needed it, and who saved the life of a young German man who may not have made it through the night without him.

Annemarie Hartnett

First published in 2006, Annemarie Hartnett has written stories under various pseudonyms in just about every genre. Her young adult historical romance set during the Halifax Explosion can currently be read at www.shadowsmayfall.com. A Mount Saint Vincent University graduate, she grew up in Halifax, where she still lives, and works in the non-profit sector.

Find more about her writing and what she's working on next by visiting her website at www.annemariehartnett.com.

The Halifax Explosion

Diana Tibert

A personal perspective...

As a child growing up in Cole Harbour, Halifax County, Nova Scotia, only a 20-minute drive to Halifax, I learned about the Halifax Explosion at an early age at school. I also heard family and friends talk about it. What I didn't know as a young girl was the scope of devastation and the number of people it impacted locally, across Canada and elsewhere.

Hubert Frank Appleby

My mother's father, Hubert Frank Appleby, arrived in Halifax in 1919, shortly after the First World War had ended. He had served overseas with the Canadian Expeditionary Force and disembarked at the port city to be discharged before returning home to Burin, Newfoundland. The city had only begun to recover, according to him, and the unsightly landscape and poor conditions left a sour impression in his memory.

When his daughter—my mother—planned to come to Halifax in 1945 while she awaited a visa to move to the United States, this memory returned and he warned her it was an unfit city. She was to stay with his brother's family,

147

and he gave her strict instructions she was to leave when her visa arrived.

My mother didn't head his warning and worked for four years in the cafeteria of Dalhousie before meeting and marrying my father, a bluenoser who had also returned from overseas from a different war with the same enemy. The couple lived in the city for two years before moving to Dartmouth and eventually Cole Harbour. Their impression of the city was drastically different from that of my grandfather who did not return to Nova Scotia until the 1970s.

Those growing up in Nova Scotia have their own stories to share with connections to the Explosion. Although my family has been in the province for more than 260 years and my mother's uncle lived on Yukon Street, Halifax, in 1917, we were fortunate no one was killed in the disaster. I do not even have a record of anyone being injured. This can't be said for many other families that lived here during that time.

The unprecedented disaster...

On August 4, 1914, Canada joined allied forces and went to war with the Central Powers in Europe (Germany, Austria-Hungary and Turkey). The ice-free harbour of Halifax was strategically located, making it a vital link to the conflict overseas. It was the perfect staging area for trans-Atlantic convoys. Military personnel from across the country congregated in Halifax and Dartmouth. They either prepared for transport overseas or remained at military facilities to help with the war effort on this side of the Atlantic. Hospital ships arrived at the port, bringing war-torn troops from Britain to home. Civilian men and women also came for many reasons, including to work as labourers.

The many military ships, merchant vessels and other types of watercraft created heavy traffic in Halifax Harbour. Add to this the types of cargo transported, such as fuel, ammunition and explosives, made it a recipe for disaster.

On the morning of December 6, 1917, a cataclysmic event struck, leaving large sections of Halifax and Dartmouth in ruins.

It would go down in history as the largest man-made explosion of its time and would remain number one on the list until the atomic bomb in 1945.

The SS *Imo*, a Norwegian vessel chartered to transport relief supplies overseas, struck the SS *Mont-Blanc*, a French cargo ship on route from New York to France. Loaded with wartime explosives, the *Mont-Blanc* caught fire. It raged out of control and ignited the cargo. The resulting catastrophic blast obliterated nearly every structure within a half mile. The pressure wave inflicted major damage at points well beyond that. The blast created a tsunami that destroyed what the Explosion had left standing in the Mi'kmaq community at Turtle Grove and tossed the British ship *Curaca* upon its shore. On board the ship, 45 crewmembers died.

At Turtle Cove, the destruction from the blast and wave were complete. "When J. H. Mitchell of the Halifax Disaster Record Office visited the settlement some days later, he described the devastation as 'incomprehensible'. Nothing, not even the pines that used to shade the houses, remained standing. 'Everything

Image #02 The Tufts Cove School was extensively damaged in the Explosion. The school was located at the northeast corner of Albro Lake Road and Windmill Road, Tufts Cove, Dartmouth.

is gone,' Mitchell wrote. 'Of some houses there is absolutely no vestige, not even of ashes...Clothing, furniture, stoves, trunks, etc., are everywhere'. Nine of the twenty-one residents of Turtle Cove died in the Explosion; the rest were seriously wounded." [*The Halifax Explosion: Heroes and Survivors* by Joyce Glasner, page 116]

More than 2,000 people were killed and another 9,000 were injured because of the Explosion, tsunami, building collapses and fires. Many people died instantly from the force of the Explosion or from flying debris.

Image #03 The SS *Imo*, the Norwegian vessel chartered to transport relief supplies overseas that struck the SS Mont-Blanc. It was driven ashore and was severely damaged. The bridge and deck crew were killed.

The flying pieces of wreckage were deadly and maimed thousands, and it needs defining in its own right. Anyone within a certain radius at the moment of the Explosion was struck with debris from the blast. Those outdoors a moment afterwards were inundated with falling objects ranging in size from particles of sand to heavy pieces of equipment. The objects—both falling and flying—moved so fast, they cut holes into flesh, removed limbs and decapitated. Objects coming from near the centre of the Explosion were molten hot.

"Red-hot rivets and other small pieces of debris fell among (sic) them and ploughed into the earth, missing the prostrate bodies by inches. Then, with a crash, a larger section of the

Mont Blanc's (sic) boiler hit the roof of the college and ripped downward through the upper floor into Study 8 where it shattered the master's dais and splintered the empty desks." [*The Town that Died* by Michael J. Bird, page 68]

Amongst those who died were individuals who had initially survived the blast and fires but succumbed to frigid temperatures and the blizzard that moved into Halifax that evening while they awaited rescue. Many of those blown into the harbour or swept away by the tsunami died from hyperthermia and drowning.

The people who survived the Explosion and who were close enough to feel its force, were stripped of much or all of their clothing and splattered with oil and dirt. They wandered in a daze, trying to find help and safety and to make sense of the bewildering event.

The number of dead impossible to count...

The official death count is 1,946. Of these, 1,631 names came from the entries entered into a special ledger-book created to record the names and details of the dead on the day of the Explosion and the days following it. The registry was closed in December 1918.

It is logical to presume that in the chaos of putting out fires, rescuing and tending to the injured and gathering the dead in short daylight hours with a blizzard on the doorstep, not all individuals were entered into the ledger. It is also logical to presume not all bodies were found. Some were more than likely burnt beyond the ability to be identified as human, and some were incinerated instantly. Others were thrown overboard and swept away while countless numbers were dragged out to sea by the tsunami. Some were simply never found in the rubble.

In a filmed interview given December 1, 1957, an unidentified fire fighter stated, "I would say at least 3,200. My reasons for that are that during that time, the rest of the winter, into the following spring, I worked with others making headboards, (undecipherable) and lumbering (hard to hear) them to place at the graves of the unidentified. Those records were kept and

Image #04 Damage from the Explosion, Halifax.

I can remember clearly that they did go over 3,200 placements. [Victims remember the tragedy of the Halifax Explosion, at 5:20 minutes]

Bird, in *The Town that Died* [page 186], added to this theory with information from possibly the same person. "Estimates of the loss of life and the total casualties in the disaster varied greatly for some time but, finally, the Halifax Relief Commission listed them as 1,963 killed, 9,000 injured and 199 blinded.

"Many people in the city, though, considered the Commission's figure for the number killed wildly inaccurate. F. C. MacGillivray, now Chief of the Halifax Fire Department, who worked with the rescuers until well into the following Spring, noted that during that time he was called upon to provide more than 3,200 markers for the dead. Few believe that the Commission took into account the fatalities on board ships in the harbour or the hundreds of citizens who disappeared without trace."

Given the large number of people who passed through Halifax and Dartmouth and who were new to the cities at this time, it is likely the number of reported missing was low in contrast to the actual number of missing. If the only people who knew an individual were killed, there'd be no one to make the report.

The tidal wave...

In Bird's book, *The Town that Died*, he stated the tsunami was 13 feet high. Other sources suggest it was as high as 60 feet in some places in the harbour. The wave was strong enough and big enough to toss around large navy ships, rip them from their moorings and destroy docks. Bird wrote, "...the wave passed on down the channel to burst over McNab's Island and then billow out into the Atlantic where some hours later and many miles out at sea, it lifted a merchant ship with such force that her captain thought she had struck a mine." [page 65]

The official time...

Perhaps we will never know. Some sources say 9:04, some say 9:05, but more say 9:06. Regardless of the time and the clocks that stopped on the second it happened, it was a crisp, late fall Thursday in December 1917.

Some miraculously escaped injury...

For no logical reason except the offer of good luck, many individuals escaped injury while others near them were injured or killed. There were many instances of clothes ripped off people without their knowledge, only to learn they walked naked in the street when someone offered them a coat. No doubt, shock had a lot to do with the lack of awareness of walking naked on a cold December day.

Due to the brave act of one man—Patrick Vincent (Vince) Coleman—approximately three hundred people travelling into Halifax by train from Saint John, New Brunswick, were saved. When the Intercolonial Railway dispatcher learned of the dangerous cargo onboard *Mont-Blanc*, he sent an emergency telegraph message to hold up the train. The train heeded the

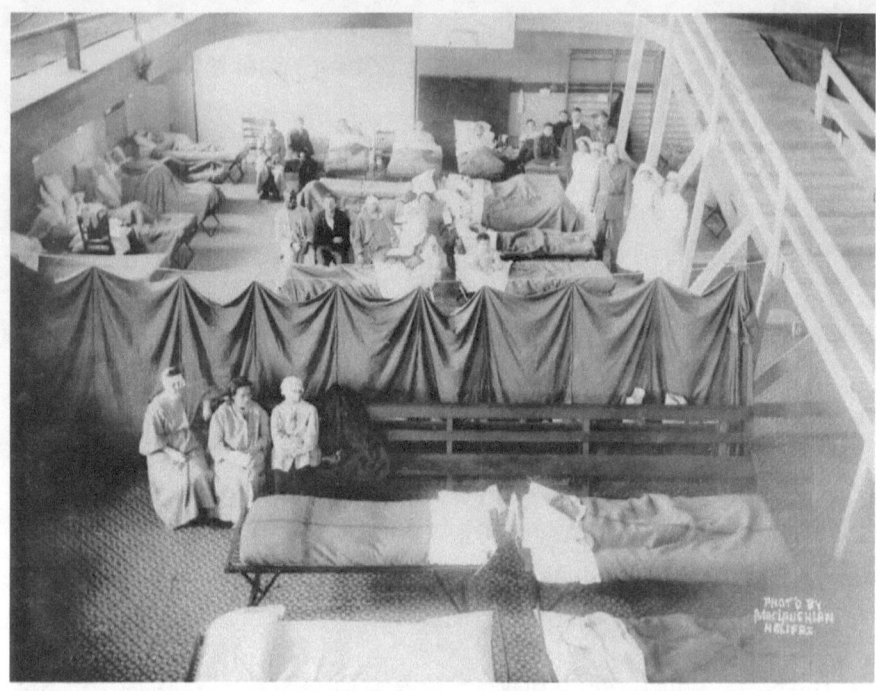

Image #05 Patients, nurses and doctors at the Emergency Relief
Hospital set up at the YMCA, Barrington Street, Halifax.

message and stopped a safe distance from the Explosion at
Rockingham, a small community leading into the centre of
Halifax.

Unfortunately, Coleman only had time to warn the train, not
to escape. He died in the Explosion.

Two thousand prized chickens at a three-day poultry show in
the City Market were unscathed though the building they were
housed was extensively damaged.

Help was on the way...

The relief effort began immediately. Those uninjured or only
slightly injured helped family, friends and strangers alike, pulling
people from burning and collapsed buildings and transporting
them to hospital. Soldiers and sailors went in to action to work
alongside civilians to save as many individuals as possible. They
worked throughout the long day and into the night, through the

cold and snow, looking for people to save and transporting the deceased to makeshift morgues.

With an important section of the tracks cleared shortly after noon on the day of the Explosion, trains began transporting the injured and homeless to places such as Truro. Those who had family elsewhere in the Maritimes were moved out over the following days to seek care and shelter from relatives to reduce the number of needy and homeless within the two cities.

Relief started arriving from other parts of Canada, Britain and the New England States within 48 hours. It came from as far away as New Zealand and China. Most notably, the people of Boston, Massachusetts, USA, and its surrounding communities rallied together to send doctors, nurses, medical supplies, money and materials to the shattered cities. Many in the state had relatives living in Nova Scotia so to them, this was personal. Many lost family members and friends.

The dark side of human behaviour...

The majority of humans are good people. When a disaster strikes, they often turn into great people and help in every manner possible. However, there are a small number of people who take advantage of opportunity and while citizens struggle to survive, the scourge of society are at work.

While citizens rushed to the Commons or to safer ground away from the shoreline for fear the Magazine would explode, looters entered homes and shops and grabbed what they could carry. They stole from the dead, taking money and personal items. In the mayhem, many escaped without arrest.

Not all looters were fortunate enough to get away. As reported in Bird's book, Mrs. Satchell, a muscular Irish woman who returned to her shop while others fled to Citadel Hill, came upon a thief robbing her establishment. She brought him down with a single blow, breaking his jaw in the process. She carried him out and threw him at the feet of a police officer.

In the days following the Explosion, looters were to be shot on sight. At least six were killed. Additional information on how authorities handled looters appeared in a Toronto newspaper. "One looter was shot, his body strapped to a post, over which was affixed a flaming legend which stated: 'This WAS a looter". [*The Town that Died*, Bird, page 132]

Although some might dismiss these types of reports to sugarcoat an already horrible event, witnesses to such punishments told similar stories to that in the newspaper. One looter was said to be nailed to a door as a warning to would-be thieves.

Spreading fear and rumours...

Immediately after the Explosion, those who did not know the true hazards of the fire on the *Mont-Blanc* blamed the Germans. They were the enemy and Canada was fighting them overseas. German U-boats were spotted off the coast and they were suspects in the disappearing fishing vessels out of Newfoundland. Fear-fueled hate spread throughout the cities and groups of individuals targeted German citizens.

On December 10th, the police were instructed by the military to arrest every German resident. This added fuel to the rumours the Germans were responsible for the Explosion. Media outlets added their own gas to the 'place the blame' fires with sensational headlines for the "Hate the Hometown Hun" campaign: "WE NOW KNOW, TOO, THAT THE PRIME RESPONSIBILITY for this, as for every other catastrophe which has afflicted the peoples of the earth as a by-product of the war, rests with that close co-partner, that arch fiend, the Emperor of the Germans." [*The Town that Died*, Bird, page 160] The newspaper claimed the Germans who lived amongst them who enjoyed their freedom have repaid the kindness the "PAST FEW DAYS BY LAUGHING OPENING AT OUR DISTRESS AND MOCKING OUR SORROW." [*The Town that Died*, Bird, page 161]

Nothing could have been further from the truth.

The small population of Germans living within Halifax and Dartmouth feared for their lives and liberty, and many remained quietly hidden or left the city for fear of retribution.

Finding more information about the Explosion...

There are numerous resources online, in print and at the public archives to help researchers and interested individuals learn more about the Explosion. A simple Google (https://www. google.ca) search will uncover thousands of pages and images.

Image #06 City of Tents set up to accommodate the homeless

Online Resources

The Nova Scotia Archives (http://novascotia.ca/archives/virtual/?Search=THexp&List=all) The site features many personal narratives and other materials connected with the Halifax Explosion. Included in the personal narratives is a letter from Ethel Jane Bond (born 1888) to her uncle Murray Kellough located in Winnipeg, Manitoba, dated December 16, 1917. It describes in detail the devastation, the death of her father, the injuries of her sister and the impact on their neighbours.

The Halifax Explosion Film is a thirteen-minute black and white film shot by professional cameraman W. G. MacLaughlan. The silence of the film adds an eerie feeling to the images as MacLaughlan captures the devastation of the city in the days immediately following the Explosion.

Halifax Explosion Remembrance Book
(https://novascotia.ca/archives/remembrance)
The online database contains the list of the dead. It includes name, place of residence, age, date of death and other pertinent information.

Maritime Museum of the Atlantic
(https://maritimemuseum.novascotia.ca/what-see-do/halifax-explosion)

List of Ships involved in the Explosion
(https://maritimemuseum.novascotia.ca/research/ships-halifax-explosion)
The webpage tells about the ships in the harbour, any damaged suffered and their role in the rescue.

100 Year – 100 Stories
(https://100years100stories.ca)

Nova Scotia Historical Vital Records
(https://www.novascotiagenealogy.com)
Search for death records of those who perished in the disaster.

Nonfiction Books

Survivors: Children of the Halifax Explosion
    by Janet Kitz (2000)
The Halifax Explosion: Heroes and Survivors
    by Joyce Glasner (2011)
The Town that Died
    by Michael J. Bird (1962)

Fiction Books

Burden of Desire
    by Robert MacNeil (1992)
Tides of Honour
    by Genevieve Graham (2015)
Who's a Scaredy Cat! A Story of the Halifax Explosion
    by Joan Payzant (1992)

Images

Image #01 (front of book) Explosion Blast Cloud
Date: December 6, 1917
Source: Wikimedia Commons
Author: Unknown
Copyright: This Canadian work is in the public domain in Canada.

Image #02 (page 149) Tufts School Damage
Date: between 1917 and 1918
Source: Wikimedia Commons
Author: Unknown
Copyright: This Canadian work is in the public domain in Canada.

Image #03 (page 150) SS *Imo* blown ashore
Date: December 1917
Source: Wikimedia Commons
Author: Unknown
Copyright: This Canadian work is in the public domain in Canada.

Image #04 (page 152) House damage from the Explosion, Halifax.
Date: 1917 - 1918
Source: Wikimedia Commons
Author: Unknown
Copyright: This Canadian work is in the public domain in Canada.

Image #05 (page 154)
Emergency Relief Hospital, YMCA, Barrington Street, Halifax
Date: December 1917-18
Source: Wikimedia Commons
Author: W.G. MacLaughlan
Copyright: This Canadian work is in the public domain in Canada.

Image #06 (page 157) City of Tents
Date: January 5, 1918
Source: Wikimedia Commons
Author: Unknown
Copyright: This Canadian work is in the public domain in Canada.